Roxy
S

Jan 2018
19

Three Ring Threat

Donna Kelly

Annie's®
AnniesFiction.com

Library of Congress-in-Publication Data
Three Ring Threat / by Donna Kelly
p. cm.
I. Title
2017956012

AnniesFiction.com
(800) 282-6643
Antique Shop Mysteries™
Series Creator: Shari Lohner
Series Editor: Elizabeth Morrissey
Cover Illustrator: Bonnie Leick

10 11 12 13 14 | Printed in China | 9 8 7 6 5 4 3 2 1

1

Maggie Watson leaned forward in the driver's seat of her Jetta and studied the sugar maple in front of her, its enormous gnarled branches reaching toward the bright-blue sky in a burst of copper, yellow, and bright red. "Looks like the perfect climbing tree."

"We called it our memory tree," Ina Linton said, peering out the passenger-side window. Her voice was distant, almost child-like. "Hattie and I climbed that tree every chance we could get."

Maggie smiled as her friend's soft, cotton-white hair lifted in the breeze. "I'll bet the leaves of that tree have rustled with a fair share of whispered secrets."

"Indeed. I've watched three generations of Hattie Wyeth's family—well, she used to be Hattie Fredricks—and their friends take shelter under it. Her father and uncles climbed, hid, and played among those branches long before we ever did, and we used to sit on the porch and talk while her youngsters discovered its secrets." Ina turned to Maggie, who was startled to see her bright-blue eyes darkened by tears. "I can hardly believe Hattie is gone and her daughter is selling the place."

Maggie put her hand on Ina's forearm and glanced down at her skin. Her smooth hands didn't look like they belonged on a woman in her midseventies. "I know this is a tough time. I'm glad I can be here for you."

Ina's lips curved into a small smile. "I'm glad Shelley is giving you first dibs on Hattie's antiques. It helps to know you'll be shepherding them to their next home."

"What a lovely way to put it." Silence fell between them,

but Ina's eyes held a small twinkle through the veil of sadness. *Leave it to Ina to think of the well-being of her friend's antiques,* Maggie thought.

Even before Maggie inherited Sedgwick Manor and the adjacent Carriage House Antiques shop from her aunt Evelyn, she'd been fascinated by the stories and mysteries surrounding the families who had once owned the heirlooms. She cherished the idea of safeguarding a family's treasures until they became a part of someone else's history.

Maggie squeezed Ina's arm. "Are you ready to go in?"

"Ready as I'll ever be," Ina said, grabbing her canvas tote bag and opening the car door. "There's no telling what Hattie left for me. Shelley said she didn't open the box since it was sealed with packing tape and had 'For Ina Linton' written on the top. I half-expect a toy snake to pop out when I open the lid. Hattie was such a card."

They walked in silence on a carpet of maple leaves that covered the brick path to the pristine forest-green Victorian home with russet accents. Ina stopped halfway to the front porch and looked up. "Hattie's bedroom was in the turret when we were kids. I always loved how we could see out of her room on three sides."

The breeze kicked up and showered more leaves onto the path as Maggie took Ina's arm and led her to the porch. The door opened as they reached the top step.

"Hi, ladies. Come in." Shelley Wyeth Mooreland wrapped Ina into a hug. "It's good to see you, Ina. I know you miss Mom as much as I do."

Ina's head bobbed. "That I do."

Shelley led them through a small foyer into a cozy parlor decorated in hues of rose and beige. "The box Mom left you is in here," she said.

Maggie looked around in admiration. Three porcelain dancers

in Victorian dress seemed to glide across the white fireplace mantel. In the sitting area, a beige Queen Anne love seat was flanked by two matching chairs accented with needlepoint floral pillows. A file storage box, its lid secured with a band of packing tape, rested on an old wooden steamer trunk in front of them.

Ina approached the trunk and stared down at the box, her hands toying with the zipper on her jacket. Her open, weathered face was atypically unreadable.

"Make yourselves comfortable," Shelley said, sitting down in a chair. "I put a pair of scissors by the box for you, Ina."

Ina continued to gaze at the box without opening it. Maggie had never before seen her so pensive. "Ina," she said, sitting down on the love seat. "Are you okay?"

"What?" Ina looked up and blinked. "Oh, yes. I'm all right." She sat on the edge of the love seat with her tote bag at her feet, picked up the scissors, and sliced through the tape holding the box closed. Taking a deep breath, Ina lifted the lid and peered inside. "Oh my goodness, my box camera," she said, lifting what appeared to be a cube with a lens and holding it in the air. "I can't believe she kept it all these years."

Maggie leaned closer to the clunky, boxy object Ina held with reverence between the palms of her hands. "Cameras sure have changed a bit in the last sixty years."

"Like everything else." Ina placed the camera on her lap and caressed it with her fingers. "This was under the Christmas tree in 1954. My first camera." She grinned like a child. "I took photos everywhere I went. By the time I was in high school, the editor of *The Somerset Harbor Herald* was publishing them in the paper. This old camera put me on the path to becoming a professional photographer."

Maggie arched her eyebrows. "I didn't know you were a professional photographer."

"I was, for a time. Those were some of the best years of my life." Ina placed the camera on the trunk. "When I was in college, my father gave me a better camera, and I passed this one to Hattie."

She reached into the box and fished out a tiny yellow container with a brown lid. "Wow, I haven't seen one of these in a while."

Shelley leaned forward, her long brown hair spilling over her shoulders. "What is it?"

"A film canister." Ina shook it, furrowing her brows. "Sounds like there's a roll inside. Why on earth would she have kept it all these years?" She rummaged through the box, lifting items out one by one and quickly replacing them with barely a glance.

Maggie caught a glimpse of a faded event ticket as well as a circus program sporting pictures of a lion and tamer, a scantily clad trapeze artist, and a beautiful woman on horseback. The box also contained a poster that Ina unrolled and rerolled so quickly Maggie couldn't see the design.

"Alrighty then," Ina said, pressing the lid on the box. "Now, let's check out your antiques."

Maggie's eyes were glued to the box lid. "I'd really like to get a peek at the circus program. May I look at it?"

"Now?"

"Just for a minute."

Ina's sigh was audible as she lifted the lid and yanked the program from the box. "I'll put it in my bag so it will be handy for you to see it later," she said, shoving the program between the canvas sides. "We have antiques to check out."

Maggie rose to her feet and resisted the temptation to ask why Ina was in such a hurry. She turned to Shelley. "I appreciate you offering us the first look."

"Certainly," Shelley said, standing. "Mom loved your aunt Evelyn and Carriage House Antiques. She'd want you to be in charge of finding new homes for her treasures."

The trio filed into the hallway with Shelley in the lead.

"As we went through Mom's stuff, I set aside some small items I thought you might like." Shelley stopped at a long drop-leaf table nestled along the wall opposite the stairs. It held several objects: a charming oil lamp with a hand-painted porcelain base and a clear glass chimney, a pair of stunning silver candelabra featuring intricate scrollwork, and a gorgeous 1930s table lamp with a fringed half-moon silk shade. A three-tier wicker sewing basket was perched on the floor beside it.

"Oh, I love all of these." Maggie eyed each one and considered whether or not it was suitable for Carriage House Antiques. She leaned over to study the table lamp. The floral, berry, and butterfly design on the shade was accented with beaded fringe along the bottom edge. The base featured two stem-like pieces curling from the main post into two bursts of white flowers. "This lamp is especially unique. Do you have a price list?"

"We can talk prices after you have a chance to see everything." Shelley waved her hand toward a door on the other side of the hallway table. "There are a couple of things in the library you might like."

Maggie stopped in the doorway and looked into the room, which appeared to be designed for music lovers and bibliophiles alike. At the far end, a baby grand piano and a pedal harp flanked a large window dressed in velvet drapes. Built-in shelving—packed with books and a smattering of framed family photos—covered the two side walls. A cozy seating area filled one corner. "What a lovely space."

Shelley walked to the sitting area and placed her hand on the back of a heavy throne-like chair with burgundy leather cushions covering the back and seat. It featured thick bands of ornately carved wood on both sides of the back and had arm posts to match. "This is one of the most unusual pieces in the house. It's a—"

"Victorian game chair," Ina finished for her. "I was enthralled with its drawers and hidden compartments as a child." Her eyes glinted like sapphires as she divulged the chair's secrets. First, she pulled a drawer built into the chair's right arm post. "Decks of cards were kept in here, but we hid messages in the tiny space behind it." She pulled on the center of a flower carved into the chair below the drawer and opened a second drawer. "Chess pieces were in here. Beautiful hand-carved pieces in ebony and boxwood that belonged to Hattie's grandfather." She tugged at another carved flower and opened a drawer located below the seat. "The chessboard was hidden here."

"It certainly is unusual. The carved design is gorgeous too." Maggie smiled, but it was as much for her friend's exuberance as for the interesting chair. Ina was acting more like herself.

Shelley peeked at her watch and approached what looked like a disembodied flight of stairs resting next to one of the bookshelves. "I thought you might be interested in the library steps. They're mahogany, mid-1800s."

Maggie was tempted to keep these for herself. Supported by carved posts in the back, the mahogany stairs were flanked by wood flourishes on each side. "I might have a difficult time letting those go. They're striking."

"I understand. I'd keep them if my husband and I had a library in our apartment in Portland." Shelley turned to the door. "Our last stop is Mom's office in the turret."

The three women filed up the stairs and turned into the turret room.

Ina took three steps into the room and stopped. "This was Hattie's favorite place in the house." Her voice cracked with emotion. "After she married Joseph and Shelley was born, Hattie turned this room into her office. We always took our tea in here."

Here, Hattie Wyeth's quirky-but-impeccable taste was most

evident. The furnishings played off the room's curved walls, particularly the tufted leather conversation sofa and an octagonal Victorian aquarium turned into a fantasy-themed terrarium. A Victorian burl walnut writing desk faced the window, near a self-standing circular bookcase. Maggie was interested in them all.

"We're keeping the two leather chairs and the circular bookcase, but you're welcome to the other items. We simply don't have the space." Shelley looked at her watch again. "I'm sorry to rush you, but the real estate agent is due here in a few minutes."

Maggie spied two slender rectangular boxes resting on an ottoman in front of one of the chairs. "What's in the boxes?"

"Oh, I almost forgot to tell you about them," Shelley said. She rubbed her temples. "Selling Mom's house must be getting to me. Those are photo boxes. I culled the most meaningful family photos to keep, but I thought you might want a few of the others. Why don't you look at them while I go downstairs and work up prices on the items you like?"

"I'll take everything you showed me. They're all gorgeous pieces."

"Excellent. I'll be right back with an invoice."

Alone in the turret, Maggie and Ina sifted through the photo boxes and selected a dozen photos representing life in Somerset Harbor in the middle of the twentieth century: exuberant soldiers in uniform returning from World War II, Hattie's father as mayor opening the door to the newly rebuilt high school in the 1950s, and streetscapes of downtown at Christmastime in the 1960s. Ina held Maggie spellbound with memories of her younger days as they dug through the box.

"It's funny," Ina said, replacing the lids on the photo boxes. "Although Somerset Harbor kept up with technology, it managed to retain its charm. I like that."

"Me too." Maggie stacked the photos she selected in a neat pile on the table as Shelley walked through the door.

"Here you go." Shelley held out a sheet of paper to Maggie. "I think you'll find these figures reasonable."

Maggie scanned to the bottom line and found a figure so reasonable it didn't demand haggling. "I'm fine with this. I'd like to add a dozen photos to the list as well."

"How about five dollars for the dozen?"

"Sold." Maggie pulled out her checkbook. "I'll write you a check now. We can arrange a time for pickup later."

Maggie handed a check to Shelley. As they made their way back downstairs, Ina took one last glance into the house where she'd spent countless hours of her childhood. Then they crossed the threshold to the porch.

"What a lovely old home," Maggie said, breaking the silence halfway down the front walk as she paused to shift Ina's box in her arms. "So many people have laughed and cried there. It's almost as if the house has a soul. In a way, it's like this box—holding your memories all these years."

Ina looked at Maggie as if she'd just said she believed in ghosts. "That was a long time ago."

"It's good to hold on to memories." Maggie resumed the trek to the car.

"Not all of them."

Maggie waited for Ina to explain, but she remained silent the rest of the way to the Jetta. Balancing the box on one hip, Maggie opened the trunk. "Do you have time for us to stop by the historical society museum before I take you home?" She lowered Ina's box of memorabilia into the trunk. "I'd like to give Ruth the photos I bought. She'll be thrilled."

Ina chuckled. "She sure will. Ruth takes her duties as president of the historical society very seriously."

"Indeed," Maggie said. "She keeps the museum in tip-top shape."

"You know, we should ask if Shelley would be willing to

donate the rest of the photos she doesn't want to keep for herself," Ina suggested. "I'm sure she'd be happy to do it, and there must be a ton of history in those pictures."

"Good idea." Maggie walked to the driver's side of the car and slid behind the wheel as Ina climbed into the passenger seat.

"I'm always up for a trip to the museum," Ina said, closing the door. "Besides, I'm grateful for the ride to Hattie's place. That box would have been a bear to lug all the way home. I'm happy to tag along wherever you need to go. One never knows where the next adventure awaits."

Maggie turned the key in the ignition and toyed with the idea of asking Ina the question she'd pondered ever since meeting her. *Why doesn't a strong, independent woman like Ina drive?*

"I'm glad I could help. Besides, I enjoy your company." Maggie took a deep breath and counted to ten while she released it. "Ina, I've always wondered . . ."

She paused. *Will Ina think I'm being invasive?*

"Well, out with it," Ina urged. "What have you always wondered?"

Maggie drummed her fingertips on the steering wheel and gathered her courage. She turned her head toward her friend. "Why don't you drive?"

A deafening silence filled the air. Maggie regretted asking the question. *Is it too late to retract it?*

"I just don't." Ina set her chin, her voice firm but not angry. "That's all."

"I'm sorry for prying." Reluctant to look at Ina, Maggie turned toward the road to check for oncoming cars. Seeing none, she pulled away from the curb.

"You don't have to apologize, but there's nothing really to discuss." Ina patted her white cottony curls, loosened by the breeze. "I wonder if Ruth will create a display of Hattie's old photos. Her grandfather owned and operated the town pharmacy back in the day. He served as mayor, as did Hattie's father. They were pretty important."

Maggie managed a smile. *Nice subject change. Message received loud and clear.* "I wouldn't be surprised. Ruth is always up for a new display project."

As the car came to a stop in front of the museum, a suit-clad, slender man with short brown hair and a mustache burst through the front door and bounded down the steps of the teal-and-rose Victorian house.

"Wonder where he's going in such a rush," Ina said, twisting in her seat to watch him lope around the corner. "Young people are always in such a hurry these days."

Maggie restrained a chuckle. The man had looked to be in his forties, like her. "Life is busier these days. And might I add you're one of the busiest people I know."

"You know the proverb, 'Idle hands are the devil's workshop,'" Ina quoted, opening her car door.

Relieved the tension between them was broken, Maggie joined Ina on the sidewalk. They strolled up the walkway to the painted lady that held the historical society museum. Maggie loved the old house, especially the white gingerbread trim. Though not as large as many of Somerset Harbor's old homes, it had its fair share of charm.

They found Ruth in the front room, adjusting an old football uniform on a mannequin. "Isn't this neat? Patrice Ramsell was cleaning out her attic and found a uniform worn by her grandfather back in the 1940s." Ruth pushed up the sleeves of the old jersey and stepped back to check out the results. "I thought it'd make a nifty display to kick off football season. We have some old photos from football games in the archives. I'll dig them out."

Ina studied the football uniform. "Are you going to round

up a vintage cheerleading uniform too? Someone's bound to have one."

"I'll ask around. I suppose cheerleaders should get equal billing." Ruth pulled off her tortoiseshell glasses and rubbed the lenses with the hem of her shirt. "What brings you two by?"

"I purchased several items from Hattie Wyeth's home, including these," Maggie said, pulling the packet of photos from her purse. "They're a random collection of photos that appear to have been taken between 1940 and the early 1960s. I thought you might like them for the museum's archives."

Ruth nestled her glasses on her face, then took the brown packet from Maggie's outstretched hand. "Any photos of the circus?"

"I didn't see any. Why?" Maggie said, as Ina drifted over to the football display and brushed a bit of lint from the jersey's sleeve.

"While I was trying to finish the display, two men came in, one right after the other, and asked for information and photos from past circus performances." Ruth shrugged. "They must have been inspired by the posters popping up all over town announcing the impending arrival of Circus de Vita."

"Hey, know what would be neat with this display?" Ina said, walking around the mannequin. "Game programs, tickets, pom-poms, and megaphones."

Ruth snickered. "She doesn't give up, does she?"

"Not easily, anyway." Maggie chuckled and glanced at her watch. "I need to take Ina home and get back to the shop. Good luck with the display."

"Thanks for the photos. I'll have fun looking through them."

Maggie and Ruth ambled over to the football display.

"I promise to look for cheerleading memorabilia," Ruth said, placing a hand on Ina's shoulder.

Ina grinned. "Cheerleaders everywhere will applaud you."

Maggie opened the door to the museum, and she and Ina stepped into the sunshine. Her cell phone rang as they reached the car. She pulled the phone from her purse and checked the screen. "It's James," Maggie said, placing the phone to her ear. "Good morning, James. How are you?"

"I'm busy, but in a good way. I've got a new project I'm working on with a highly respected interior designer and space planner." His voice was laced with excitement. "I'd like to drop by Carriage House Antiques and introduce you to her."

"Now?"

"In about fifteen minutes. We're finishing a late breakfast at the Oceanview Hotel."

A pretty fancy place for a working meal. "I'll meet you at the shop after I take Ina home."

"Sounds good. See you then."

Maggie ended the call. "That's weird," she said, pointing her key fob at the car. "James seemed almost giddy about bringing this lady, his new colleague, by the shop."

"That certainly is odd," Ina said, her eyes brimming with mischief. "And there's no way I'm going home now. I want to meet this mystery woman."

"She's a colleague, not a mystery woman," Maggie said, pulling away from the curb a bit faster than usual.

But why did James sound so eager for me to meet her?

2

A melodic laugh danced across Carriage House Antiques as Maggie and Ina hung their jackets on the wood peg by the door. They followed the laughter and found June McGillis, the shop manager, watching with raised eyebrows as a statuesque woman tossed auburn locks over her shoulder and leaned on James's arm.

"Oh James, of course art nouveau isn't suitable for the Witmarsh Mansion. It's simply too whimsical for the Federal-style architecture of the place." The redhead batted her eyelashes and tapped a French-manicured fingernail on his forearm. A black designer handbag dangled from the crook of her other arm. "But it would be perfect for my client who lives in a quirky loft in SoHo. Manhattan, that is, not London."

"My mistake," James said, extricating himself from the redhead's grip as Maggie and Ina joined the trio. He waved and smiled in greeting. "Maggie, Ina, how are you?"

Maggie stole a quick glance at his face. *Is James blushing?* She held her hand out to the stranger. "Hi, I'm Maggie Watson."

"Juliet Caulfield." The woman's handshake was firm, confident. "James tells me you and June will be invaluable contacts while we're working on the Witmarsh Mansion."

"June and I are happy to help you in any way we can." Maggie studied the way Juliet's deep burgundy-and-gray silk blouse flowed easily over her gray trousers. The stiletto heels on her boots could have been used as weapons. Maggie pulled at the hem of her sweater, which seemed a bit less fashionable than it had that morning. "Please let us know what you need."

Ina waved her hand in salute. "I'm Ina Linton, tagalong." She stared at Juliet's feet. "Impressive boots. How do you walk in them?"

"You get used to it. I've been wearing stilettos since I was sixteen years old. To me, they're more comfortable than running shoes." Juliet eyed the Seth Thomas clock on the wall. "I'm afraid we don't have much time at the moment, but I'd like to take a quick walk-through to get a feel for the rest of your shop."

June toyed with the cloisonné pen dangling from her neck on a chain. "Walk this way, and I'll give you the ten-cent tour. You'll find unique pieces from a variety of time periods. We're blessed with fairly rapid turnover most of the time."

With Maggie and Ina lingering behind and watching, Juliet took James's arm and followed June past several displays, stopping from time to time to consult on specific pieces for their project.

"She's standing so close to him it looks like she's nibbling his ear," Ina whispered as Juliet and James studied a pair of ornamental statues suitable for a formal garden. "In my day, women played a little harder to get."

Strange electricity flashed through Maggie as James stopped, pointed at an intricate detail on an angel statue, and looked at Juliet. Maggie clutched her purse with a death grip. "He seems to like it."

Ina chuckled. "I guess any man would"—she paused for effect—"if he wasn't into subtle flirting."

"Oh, Ina." Maggie slapped her friend's wrist lightly, a barely audible laugh escaping her lips despite her attempt to restrain it.

As the group finished the tour and returned to the front counter, a chime sounded from Juliet's bag. "This must be our reminder to head back to Witmarsh Mansion." She reached into her purse, pulled out a jeweled card case, and opened it. "James is right. You have a beautiful shop. Here's my card." She passed the thick ivory card to Maggie with two long, thin fingers. "I'll be in touch."

Maggie snagged a business card from the milk glass sugar bowl that served as her card holder, paused to scribble her cell phone number on the back with the desk pen, and handed it to Juliet. "Feel free to call anytime. We're always bringing in new items. June and I stay on the lookout for unusual, quality pieces."

"I'm sure you do," Juliet said, plucking the card from Maggie's fingers. "We'll talk soon."

James put his hand on Maggie's arm. "It was good to see you, Maggie."

"Thank you for recommending Carriage House Antiques to Juliet," she replied, hoping she sounded cool and composed. "I think the connection will be good for both of us."

He glanced at Juliet, who was standing by the shop exit with one hand on the knob and one foot tapping impatiently. "She's certainly good at what she does," James said, then joined Juliet at the door.

June, Maggie, and Ina watched in silence as the pair left the shop.

"What would she know about running shoes? I'm pretty sure Juliet Caulfield has never run a day in her life," Ina muttered as soon as the shop door closed behind them. "Unless it was to beat the crowds at Neiman Marcus."

June chuckled. "Regardless, she must be good at design if she's working on Witmarsh Mansion. Helene and Cecil Witmarsh are accustomed to the best money can buy." June tucked a lock of hair behind her ear. "Evelyn and I were fortunate to work with the designer they flew in from New York when they refurbished their guest cottage ten years ago. No expense was spared to find the perfect furnishings."

"Knowing the Witmarshes' reputation for tasteful extravagance,

I'm sure this time will be no different," Ina said. She prided herself on being a walking encyclopedia of Somerset Harbor families. "Getting to know Ms. Caulfield could be good for business."

June's head bobbed in agreement. "I only hope James survives unscathed. She certainly has the personality traits of a man-eater."

A strange twinge flickered through Maggie as she lifted her jacket off the peg. "James is a grown man. I'm sure he can take care of himself."

When she turned back around, she saw Ina and June exchange quick glances. She frowned. "Can we get to work, please?"

· · · · · · · · · · · · · · · · · ·

"Stopping for lunch seemed like a good idea when you suggested it," Ina said, searching for a table inside The Busy Bean. She clutched her bag—which now held the old circus program in addition to her customary miniature flashlight and microcamera—close to her side. "Today this place is living up to its name."

"True. I guess the cooler weather has people wanting more coffee," Maggie said, scanning the room for an empty table. Jenny and Bethany, the café's friendly waitresses, scurried from table to table like bees darting from one flower to another. The dining room hummed with voices and the clatter of silverware on dishes. By the window, a man tapped on a laptop. With his head bent toward the screen and his face partially obscured by his longish wavy brown hair, he was oblivious to the noise inside and the view of the streetscape outside.

A gray-haired couple at the next window-side table pushed back their chairs and stood up.

"Look, that couple is vacating a table." Maggie glanced at the checkout counter and waved to Daisy Carter, the café's owner, who was handing change to a customer.

Daisy nodded and lifted her hand in a beauty queen wave, a habit left over from her year as Miss Savannah when she was a teenager. "I'll be over in a minute," she called.

Maggie and Ina maneuvered through a maze of people en route to the empty table. The man on the computer didn't look up from the screen when Maggie brushed against his chair on her way to her seat. *What a shame. The view is a bit wasted on him.*

Ina took the chair closest to the man's table so that her back was to him. Maggie sat down across the table, the man and his laptop visible behind Ina's fluffy white curls. She set her purse on the floor next to her feet.

"Wow, what a morning." Ina hooked the handles of her bag over one side of her chair back and turned to face Maggie.

"My thought exactly." Maggie pointed to Ina's bag. "I'd like to get another look at the circus program if you don't mind." Ina's face clouded, so Maggie changed her approach. "It must have been hard for you to see Hattie's house being dismantled."

Ina twisted in her seat, reached into the bag, and pulled out the program. "It was." She placed the pamphlet on the table, her hand resting on the cover as if attempting to hold back the past. "But death is a part of life, and we figure out how to let go of people and things we love while keeping them alive in our hearts."

"Hattie must have been a dear friend to have saved your treasures all those years."

"She was the best." Ina's lips curled into a smile. "She knew my secrets. Most of them, anyway. I guess they're all safe now." Ina blinked and waved a hand. "Speaking of secrets, what do you think Juliet Caulfield is up to, manhandling James the way she did?"

"Besides excessive flirting?" Maggie snorted in an attempt to push away the awkward memory of Juliet's interaction with James. After all, she and James were friends—nothing more, nothing less. "My guess is she's seeing dollar signs in the form of clients he'll send her way."

"Whew." Daisy appeared at the table, pad and pen in hand. She gently patted her brunette bouffant hairdo, held impeccably in place by hair spray. "I'm sorry nobody's taken your order. It's been a madhouse today. Have you seen the Circus de Vita posters popping up all over the place? I think everyone's excited about the circus coming to town. They all want to come here to talk about it, which is good for me."

Ina folded her hands over the circus program, hiding the artwork on the cover. "Well, I'm here for food. My stomach's growling. I'll take the turkey club wrap and a cup of tomato bisque soup. And hot tea."

"I love a customer who knows what she wants," Daisy drawled, scribbling Ina's order on her pad. She still sounded like a Southern belle despite having lived in Somerset Harbor for the past three decades. Daisy peered at the circus program. "What have you got there?"

"Oh, this?" Ina unclasped her hands and held up the program. "Hattie Wyeth left me a box of mementos. This was one of them."

Daisy bent over to get a closer look. "A circus program from 1955. Circus de Vita, the same circus coming this week. It's a miracle the program survived, much less in such good condition. I'll bet it's worth some money."

A woman in a muumuu as bright as her red hair reached out from a nearby table and tapped Daisy on the arm. "Coffee refill?" Her voice was throaty and curt. "I've been waiting for it awhile."

"Of course, I'll be one second." Daisy flashed the woman a smile and turned to Maggie. "What can I get for you?"

"Chicken salad croissant, please, and hot tea." Maggie grinned. "I think you need a pair of roller skates today."

"I wish I'd thought of that when I got dressed this morning," Daisy said, hurrying away to the coffee station.

"Daisy might be right, you know. The circus program could be worth something." Maggie pulled the program toward her. "Want me to look into it? Or do you want to keep it for sentimental reasons?"

"I don't know." Ina shrugged. "For years, my parents, brother, and I made annual family trips to the circus, but I have plenty of other memories with them. No big deal."

But Ina's clenched jaw and drumming fingers told Maggie otherwise. *What is Ina hiding?*

Maggie's thoughts were interrupted when Daisy arrived with two cups of tea balanced in one hand and a coffeepot in the other. "Don't look now, but the gorgeous man sitting at the next table keeps eyeing you," she whispered in Maggie's ear. "I'll be back in a jiff with your lunch."

From the heat on her cheeks, Maggie imagined her face was fire-engine red. She stirred a few granules of sugar into her tea, put the cup to her lips, and peered over the rim at the man, who was indeed striking, with brown eyes and thick, chestnut-colored hair curling around his ears. He appeared to be close to her age. But instead of looking at Maggie as Daisy had suggested, he was focused on packing up his laptop.

"Daisy sent me with your order." Jenny grinned as she set two loaded plates and a soup bowl on the table. "Can I get you anything else?"

"Not for me, thanks." Maggie set to work cutting her croissant in half.

Ina dug into her wrap with the gusto of a college football player. The woman didn't do anything halfway, which Maggie had always admired about her friend.

"Excuse me, may I join you?" Maggie looked up to find the

"gorgeous man" looking down at her. He held a to-go cup, but he had left his laptop bag on the table he'd just come from.

"Sure, have a seat," Ina said while Maggie was still collecting her wits. "I'm Ina, and this is Maggie."

The man placed his cup on the table and sat down. He nodded a greeting to Maggie but addressed Ina. "I don't mean to interrupt your lunch, but I heard your conversation about the circus and wondered if you'd ever met anyone from the Circus de Vita when you were young."

"Ah, not really." Ina handed him the program. "What I know about the circus is limited to what I saw as a spectator and the information I read in the programs. Why do you ask?"

"I'm writing a book about the entertainment industry." He pulled a business card out of the breast pocket of his New York Yankees polo shirt and handed it to Ina. "Many early Hollywood actors and stuntmen started in the circus."

"'Francesco Valli, reporter. *New York Examiner.*'" Ina studied the card, then dropped it into her bag. "What brings a big-city reporter to Somerset Harbor?"

Francesco drummed his fingers on the table and stared outside. "Actually, I'm following this particular circus. Evidently, some Hollywood heavy hitters toured with them back in the day. I'm trying to figure out who they were."

"Like who?" Maggie restrained the urge to reach out and grab his hand to stop the drumming. She tore off a bit of her croissant instead and gestured toward his fingers with it. "Are you okay?" She popped the bread into her mouth and turned her head to see what was happening outside. A pair of high-end motorcycles were parked across the street, their chrome details gleaming bright.

"I'm fine. I overindulged in coffee this morning is all." His gaze continued to penetrate the window.

Ina followed his stare. "It's rare to see motorcycles in Somerset Harbor, especially with such scruffy-looking riders. Times sure are changing."

Francesco startled, his arm sending his coffee cup flying to the floor near Maggie's purse. Fortunately, the lid stayed on and the beverage didn't spill. He bent down to retrieve the cup, knocking into the purse in the process. "I'm sorry," he said, sitting up as his phone buzzed with an incoming text. He scanned the text with wide eyes. "I've got to go."

Maggie and Ina watched in stunned silence as Francesco pulled his computer bag from the next table and dashed out the door.

"Well, he was an odd fellow. Cute, but odd," Daisy said, arriving at the table and placing the check in the center of it.

"He was certainly intense." Maggie stared out the window.

The two bikers left their motorcycles and approached Francesco. They stepped in front of him, and one of the burly men placed a gloved hand on his chest to stop him.

"I'd say he was a frightened fellow." Ina reached back into her bag and pulled out a pair of mini-binoculars. Leaning toward the window, she peered through the lenses. "Hmmm, what's his story? Those guys look mighty threatening. Suppose we should call the cops?"

Before Maggie could answer, the bikers abruptly let Francesco go and returned to their motorcycles. Francesco headed back toward the café door and slipped out of view. Ina twisted in her seat, leaned toward the window, and strained to see farther down the sidewalk. "I guess not."

By the time Ina and Maggie finished their lunch, The Busy Bean was less than half-filled with customers, although the noise level was still high because two large tables remained occupied by a chatty tour group. Ina stuffed the circus program and binoculars into her bag and grabbed the check. "This one is on me. Thanks for the taxi service. No arguing."

"Twist my arm." Maggie led the way to the register, where Daisy was waiting for them.

"You had a handsome lunch companion." Daisy winked, plucking the check and cash from Ina's outstretched fingers and ringing it into the register. "Keep me posted if you hear from him again. I'll bet you do."

"You'll be the first to know," Maggie said.

"The second one to know," Ina corrected. "I expect to be the first."

Laughing at her bantering friends, Maggie pulled on the door and stepped through it. The laughter caught in her throat when she nearly tripped over Francesco, crumpled on the sidewalk. Blood seeped through the baseball insignia on his chest.

3

Maggie tore her gaze from Francesco's lifeless face and pulled her cell phone from her purse. She punched in 911, scanning the street for possible witnesses. Across the road, a blonde woman in a tan business suit calmly walked to a white SUV and climbed into the passenger side.

Maggie described the scene and their location to the dispatcher as Ina knelt to search for Francesco's pulse. After a few moments, Ina raised her face to Maggie and shook her head.

"No pulse," Maggie told the dispatcher as the white SUV pulled away from the curb. "There's a white SUV pulling out across the street."

"Can you get a plate number?" The dispatcher's tone was no-nonsense.

Maggie stepped to the curb and struggled to see the license plate as the SUV began to move, but her line of sight was cut off by a passing delivery truck. By the time Maggie had a clear view, the SUV was long gone.

"Ugh. No, a delivery truck drove by and blocked my view. I'm sorry."

"You did well. Police officers are on their way. Do you have a safe place to stay?"

Maggie noted the people gathering outside The Busy Bean. "Yes, there's quite a crowd here."

"Good. Hang tight."

Maggie ended the call, held out her hand to Ina, and pulled her friend to her feet.

"Thanks," Ina said, brushing off her slacks. "Maggie, look! Francesco's computer is gone."

Maggie closed her eyes and recounted what she remembered about the woman with the briefcase. "The lady in the SUV was tall, slender, long blonde hair, tan business suit. Briefcase, but no purse." When she opened her eyes, Ina was jotting something down on a small memo pad. "What are you doing?"

"Writing down what you said so that you can give details to the police. And I got the information off of Francesco's business card, so we'll have it after the police take the card."

Maggie smiled in spite of the stressful situation. "One never knows what you'll pull from the depths of your bag."

"Very true."

Seemingly out of nowhere, Officer Robert Linton appeared, grasped each woman by an elbow, and led Ina and Maggie away from Francesco. "Aunt Ina is always prepared, no matter where she goes. I only wish she would stay away from dead bodies."

"Will you please not talk about me like I'm not here?" Ina swatted her nephew lightly on the arm. "Besides, I like helping solve mysteries."

"He shouldn't be talking to you at all if you're involved in this homicide investigation," Officer Peter Williams said as he and his partner, Samantha Clayton, joined them. A short, stocky, balding, bulldog of a man who took his job seriously, he glared at the police officer in question. "You know you can't interview your aunt, Linton."

"I know. I heard her name over the radio. I am checking on her well-being." Close to Maggie's age, Officer Linton had a freckled face that gave him a boyish appearance. "I won't get in the way of the investigation."

True to his word, Robert stayed on the periphery of the crime scene, keeping an eye on the behavior of onlookers and the safety of Ina and Maggie. The women related their conversation with Francesco, his fixation with the bikers and subsequent conversation with them outside, and how they found him on the ground, stabbed to death, upon leaving The Busy Bean.

"Let me get this straight," Officer Williams said, skimming his notes. "Mr. Valli had a computer in his possession when he left the café, but it was missing when you found his body outside. Correct?"

Officer Clayton flipped a page on her notepad. "How long was it between the time Ms. Linton noticed the computer missing and when Mrs. Watson saw the blonde woman with the briefcase?"

Maggie replayed the scene in her mind. "I saw the woman while I was on the phone with the dispatcher. Ina realized the computer was missing right after I hung up."

Ina's nephew joined the officers, and the three exchanged glances, causing Maggie to shudder.

"You two need to be careful." Robert's eyes darkened. "You may have inadvertently witnessed a murder. Or at least a murderer leaving the crime scene. Aunt Ina, I want you to come stay at the house with us." He turned to Maggie. "It would be wise for you to call a friend to stay with you."

"Robert, that's very kind of you. Really." Ina's jaw was set. "But we are two strong, independent women. We can take care of ourselves." She nudged Maggie. "Right?"

"Right." Maggie took a deep breath. "But I promise I'll be cautious and call 911 if anything unusual happens."

Officer Clayton handed each woman a business card. "If you remember anything else, please call me."

Maggie stared at the card and couldn't help thinking of Francesco Valli's odd behavior. "I don't know if it's important, but Francesco was really fidgety. He was so nervous he knocked his coffee cup off the table. It landed near my purse. I'm lucky coffee didn't spill on it."

"I'll make a note of that," Officer Clayton said. "Thanks for your time, ladies."

Robert walked Maggie and Ina back to the car. "The department will likely have a patrol drive by your houses for a while. Stay alert and flag them down if you need anything."

After eliciting promises from them, he stood on the curb, watching them drive away until Maggie could no longer see him in the rearview mirror. A block later, a dark sedan fell in behind Maggie's Jetta. *Could this be an unmarked police car, or are we being followed by the murderer?*

Maggie took a convoluted route back to Ina's house on the off chance they were being followed, ignoring Ina's confused looks. After she had turned what should have been a three-minute drive into a twenty-minute one—and she no longer saw the sedan behind them—they finally arrived at Ina's place, a white, three-story clapboard home with a bay window. In the center of the well-kept yard, a towering oak tree sported foliage that rivaled the Wyeth sugar maple.

"Home safe and sound," Maggie said, half-expecting a police cruiser to pull in behind them. "I'll walk you inside to make sure the coast is clear."

Ina snorted. "You'll do nothing of the sort. You took so many twists and turns on the way home I almost got lost. You weren't tailed." Ina rummaged through her bag and pulled out an air horn. "Besides, if I run into hoodlums, I'll sound this little baby and blast them right out of my house. My neighbors will call the cops and come running."

Maggie grinned. Ina had more guts than anyone she knew. "I want to be you when I grow up."

"Be careful what you wish for, my dear," Ina replied, opening the door. "I'll talk to you tomorrow."

Maggie kept her eyes on Ina as the older woman walked up

the driveway and unlocked the door to the house. After Ina had waved and disappeared inside, Maggie dialed Officer Linton's phone number. She took a deep breath when he answered.

"Hi, Robert. It's Maggie." She kept her eyes on Ina's front door.

"Is everything okay?"

"Yes, I think so. I watched Ina go inside and shut the door, but we may have been followed. I took a long way to your aunt's house, and I think we lost them. It was a dark sedan. I didn't recognize it." She paused. "I thought you should know."

"Thank you. I'll have patrols watching her house and yours. Call again if you need anything, okay?"

"I promise." Maggie ended the call, put her car in reverse, and backed out of Ina's driveway. She switched on the radio in an attempt to overshadow her growing fear with the positive vibes of contemporary Christian music. The smooth voice sang of heaven, angels, and souls returning home, but the joy was tarnished when an image of Francesco's face flashed through her mind. She didn't know him, but she prayed he was in a much better place, a place without fear. *Rest in peace, Francesco. Nothing can hurt you now.*

. . . .

The next morning, Maggie sat in an overstuffed leather chair in her sitting room at Sedgwick Manor, one hand wrapped around a cup of coffee and the other stroking her tabby cat, Snickers, who purred thunderously in her lap. After a nearly sleepless night, she still couldn't quite wrap her brain around the previous day's events: the handsome reporter introducing himself, then his nervous fidgeting and questions about the circus, and finally his bleeding body crumpled on the sidewalk outside The Busy Bean.

Wanting a distraction, she set her coffee cup on the table next to her and pulled the remote control off the chair arm. Snickers, disturbed by Maggie's movement, stretched his front paws and voiced his displeasure before settling back into his curled position. When the purring resumed, Maggie pointed the remote at the television and surfed through the channels, looking for an old movie or sitcom reruns.

She flipped past the home-shopping channel, a nature show, and a 1970s action movie in which a man who looked like a young Sean Connery was jumping from one semitrailer to another on a busy highway. Nothing caught her eye until the front of The Busy Bean appeared on the screen, a photo of Francesco superimposed in the corner as a stern-faced reporter recounted the events leading up to the murder. Maggie turned up the volume.

"Why the forty-six-year-old Pulitzer Prize-winning journalist was visiting the sleepy coastal town of Somerset Harbor is unclear, although patrons in The Busy Bean claim they overheard Valli mention a book project to two women sharing a table near him." The reporter stepped aside so the cameraman could follow a couple Maggie didn't know as they approached the door and entered the café. "We understand Valli's sister is arriving here at this very moment. We'll keep you updated on this developing story. Back to you, Keith."

Anchorman Keith Jostes opened his mouth to speak, but the only noise Maggie heard was a loud banging coming from the side door of the manor. She jumped to her feet with a startled Snickers struggling in her arms. The knocking continued as she rushed through the kitchen to the sunroom door, where she found June peering through the glass pane.

June, a to-go cup in one hand, began talking as she entered the house. "I stopped by The Busy Bean for coffee on the way to work, and Daisy told me about what happened yesterday. A TV news van pulled up as I was leaving. As if that wasn't creepy enough, I arrived at the shop to find a patrol car in front." When the door closed behind her, she gave Maggie a pointed look. "Why are the police out front? I want details."

"I don't even know where to start." Maggie released the squirmy Snickers, who took off for parts unknown, and motioned for June to follow her back to the sitting room. "It was a long, strange day."

"Start with explaining why the police are outside."

"I presume the police are out front in case the person who murdered Francesco Valli comes looking for me. There's likely a patrol car outside Ina's place too. We were the last people to talk with him. But the day was weird before we made it to The Busy Bean."

June took a swig of coffee. "Did something happen when you went to see the antiques at the Wyeth house?"

"Nothing happened, exactly, it was just a little strange. Hattie had left a box for Ina, so I asked her if she wanted to come with me."

"It must have been difficult for her. I know she and Hattie were close friends."

"You know Ina. She's a trooper. She was reminiscing a lot when we first arrived at the house, but her reaction to the contents of the box was odd. She didn't say very much."

"I've never seen Ina at a loss for words." June arched her eyebrows. "What was in the box?"

Maggie shrugged. "Several little things. An old camera and circus memorabilia, mostly. Ina looked at them briefly but quickly returned them to the box and closed the lid. Then we looked at the antiques Shelley had for sale."

"Anything interesting?"

"Lots, and she gave us a good deal too." Maggie grabbed her phone off the table, opened the photo app, and passed the phone to June. "Here, take a look."

"Love the writing desk." June scrolled through the photos.

"Oh wow, this early Victorian buttoned leather conversation settee is a find. They're quite rare."

"I particularly like the library steps. I'd keep them for myself if I didn't already have a rolling ladder." Maggie smiled for the first time since leaving The Busy Bean the previous day. "I picked a few cool smaller items too. I told Shelley we'd be in touch about shipping."

"I'll take care of it." June rose to her feet. "You're getting good at finding unusual pieces and negotiating reasonable prices. Evelyn would be proud of you. She'd also tell you to be careful, especially with a murderer on the loose."

They rambled into the kitchen. Maggie stopped to pull a steak from the freezer and put it on the counter to thaw. "I have a few errands to run in town, but I'll be in public places. I want to stop by The Quilt Cupboard and get Fran's advice on repairing the antique quilt we got in that box lot last week."

"I understand," June said, following Maggie to the side door. "Just—"

"—be careful," Maggie finished for her. "I will. I promise."

. . . .

"What can I do for you, Mrs. Watson?" Paula Ellis was meticulous about her duties as the Somerset Harbor Police Department receptionist. She didn't waste time on pleasantries.

"I'd like to speak with Officer Linton, please."

"About?"

"The stabbing outside The Busy Bean."

"Do you have something new to report?"

Maggie shook her head. "I was hoping he would."

"Have a seat." Paula lifted her chin. "I'll check if he can see you."

Maggie found a chair near a potted ficus tree near the window overlooking the water. The sea, with all its ever-shifting moods, fascinated her. Relieved to focus on the waves breaking on the beach, she was vaguely aware of people entering and exiting the waiting area.

Paula's voice penetrated Maggie's thoughts. *Did she call my name?* Maggie raised her head toward the reception desk, but Paula was already escorting a woman with a graceful dancer's body into the hallway. A memory tugged at her brain. The newscast. She'd been entering The Busy Bean.

"Mrs. Watson, how are you?" Startled, Maggie looked up to find Officer Janeen Crosby looking down on her.

"A bit unsettled after yesterday, but I'm okay."

"Understandable." The officer's face softened. "Officer Linton is tied up right now, but he asked me to check on you."

"Any news?"

"I don't have the authority to talk to you about the case, and he doesn't either." Officer Crosby took a step closer to Maggie. "But he's keeping an eye on the investigation."

"I understand. Thank you for telling me." Maggie pulled her key ring from her purse.

The police officer cleared her throat. "He asked me to caution you to be extra vigilant until we have a suspect in custody. It appears we have a cold-blooded killer on the loose."

4

As Maggie exited the police station, Officer Crosby's words echoed in her mind. *Be extra vigilant.* Gazing toward the ocean, Maggie took several deep breaths. *What does that mean, anyway?*

She squared her shoulders. *Surely it doesn't mean spending my time sequestered inside the manor.* She set off in the direction of The Quilt Cupboard, appreciating the scenery on this stretch of Shoreline Drive, with the boardwalk and beach on one side and the quaint shops on the other.

She had parked her car in front of the quilt shop since it was less than a block from the police station. Reaching the Jetta, she opened the trunk and removed a tote bag holding the antique quilt she wanted advice on repairing. By the time she'd reached the shop door, Maggie's spirits had lifted a bit, knowing she was going to fix up this old quilt and salvage its history.

A bell jangled as Maggie pushed on the heavy wooden door and entered the warm, comforting atmosphere of The Quilt Cupboard. The shop—with its hardwood floors, walls dotted with colorful quilts, and antique counter and cash register—was the perfect place for her to escape the horror of the last twenty-four hours.

"Maggie, I'm glad to see you." Shop owner Fran Vosburg's quiet voice and easy manner had a calming effect. She smiled, but her dark eyes showed concern. "I heard what happened. I'm sorry you had to witness such violence yesterday. Are you okay?"

"I'm all right." Maggie held up the tote. "I'm here for a bit of quilt therapy."

Fran's dark eyes brightened. "Now you're talking." She

motioned Maggie to the counter and tilted her head toward her bag. "Show me what you have there."

For the next ten minutes, the women chatted about the best way to fix the frayed and torn areas of the otherwise well-preserved Irish chain quilt that June had thought dated to about 1890.

"You two look like you're having fun." James's voice pulled Maggie out of her repair-focused reverie.

Maggie looked up from the quilt, which was spread over the counter. James grinned at her and stepped away from Juliet's grasp. "How are you?" He pulled her into a side-arm hug and squeezed her shoulder. "We were tied up at the Witmarsh place and didn't hear the news until late last night."

"I'm fine. Nothing a bit of quilt therapy can't soothe." Maggie stepped out of his grasp as Juliet hooked her hand around his other arm. *Juliet sure keeps a tight rein on her "colleagues."*

"Oh James, look at these absolutely divine fabrics." Juliet pulled James across the shop to a rack of high-end, luxurious fabrics in deep, rich colors. She kept a grip on his arm. "Perfect. We need to get Giselle Franz in here to see these so she can get to work on the fiber art piece for the library."

"Thanks for your help." Maggie said to Fran, then began returning the old quilt to the bag, stealing a couple of glances at James and Juliet. "I'll come back if I need more advice."

"I'll be here." Fran smiled.

Across the room, Juliet was chattering about fabrics, batting her eyelashes at James each time they looked at a new bolt.

"Thanks, Fran." Maggie nodded toward James and Juliet. "I'm going to slip out without disturbing them."

Her cell phone rang as the door closed behind her. Ina's name lit up on the display screen, and she answered it as she approached her car. "Hi, Ina. How are things?"

"I can't get the murder off my mind. I walked to the historical society and helped Ruth with the cheerleader display, and we ended up talking about Francesco. On the way back, I stopped by the library and checked out an astronomy book. Of course, Maura asked me about the stabbing. When I got home, I turned on the police scanner, but nothing was happening because everyone is too busy speculating about why the reporter was murdered." Ina finally took a breath. "Maggie, we've got another mystery on our hands, and it's up to us to solve it."

Maggie slid behind the Jetta's steering wheel. "Oh yeah? And how do you propose we do that?"

"Well, for starters we can make a list of what we know and then brainstorm how to find out who killed Francesco and why. Are you in?"

"I can stop by for a bit," Maggie said, turning on the engine. "I'm just leaving The Quilt Cupboard. I'll be there in a jiff."

"Good. I'll be here with my thinking cap on."

"I have no doubt." Maggie chuckled and ended the call, then put the car in gear and pulled onto Shoreline Drive. She turned her radio to a jazz station out of Portland and relaxed as she drove the few blocks to Ina's house.

She had a feeling she wouldn't be able to relax much once she reached Ina's.

. . . .

"Hey, come on in." Ina stepped back and opened the door wider. "I fixed us some snacks to nibble while we brainstorm."

"I've never known anyone who enjoys a good mystery more than you," Maggie said, stepping over the threshold.

"I've been an amateur gumshoe since I watched Perry Mason solve crimes on television. That would have been around 1960, way before your time." Ina waved Maggie toward the kitchen.

"For me, it was *Miami Vice*," Maggie said, following Ina

into her sunny yellow-and-white kitchen. Curtains bright with red tulips danced with the breeze through the open window. "I learned cop lingo from faithfully watching Crockett and Tubbs track down the bad guys each week."

Ina's "snack" was a full-blown lunch. Two yellow Fiesta plates—each topped with a pulled pork sandwich on thick sourdough bread, sweet potato chips, and cinnamon apple slices—sat amid silverware on the red-and-chrome midcentury kitchen table. Two matching mugs, empty save tea bags waiting for steaming water, were at each place. A small pad of paper and a pen stretched horizontally above each place setting. Ina was perpetually prepared.

"Looks scrumptious." Maggie's stomach gurgled as a teakettle whistled on the stove. "My stomach definitely approves."

Ina chuckled. "I thought food would help us think."

Maggie was pleased at Ina's mirth. Neither of them had laughed much since yesterday.

"Have a seat," Ina said, grabbing the teakettle and filling each mug with water. "Time to work."

They discussed the events of the previous day, making a list of details they collectively remembered from the time they entered The Busy Bean until they drove home after the police dismissed them. The longer they talked, the more pages they filled in their notepads. Their food vanished from the plates. By the time they'd finished eating, Maggie and Ina had plenty of notes but not a solid plan of action.

"I can't make sense of notes spread over twenty small pages," Ina said, ruffling through the pages in her pad. "This is ridiculous."

"I know what you mean." Maggie sat back in her chair. "Any ideas?"

Ina propped her elbow on the table, put her chin in her hand, and closed her eyes. She sat without moving or talking for so long that Maggie considered tapping her on the shoulder to make sure she hadn't fallen asleep.

"I got it." Ina's eyes flew open. "Let's create a crime board like they do in the cop shows. Then we'll be able to visualize the relationships between people and the timing of incidents."

"Great idea." Maggie clapped her hands together as Ina held up her fist. Maggie raised her eyebrows. "What are you doing?"

"A fist bump. Come on. Put your fist up to mine. It's what all the kids do these days instead of a high five." She grinned when Maggie did as asked. "My grandnephew Bobby taught me."

"Oh, the things I learn from you, Ina Linton."

"Stick with me, kid—the learning never stops." Ina disappeared down the hallway while Maggie cleared the table and placed the dishes in the sink. She returned with a large roll of white paper, masking tape, and a package of markers.

In short order, the two women rolled out a sheet of paper and cut it to the length of the table. Ina pulled her step stool out of the corner, pushed it to the pantry door, and climbed on top of it. "Hand me the paper, then a few pieces of tape."

Maggie did as she was told. When they'd added enough tape to secure the paper to the door, Ina climbed down from the stool and stood back to survey what would be their crime board. "This will do just fine."

"Yes, it will. And I know what will make it even easier." Maggie lifted her purse from her chair back and rummaged around. "Ta-da." She pulled out a pack of sticky notes. "Here they are. My secret weapon for staying organized. We can write on these and move them around the board as needed."

"That's the spirit." Ina plucked her notepad from the table. "I say we start by chronologically listing the places we visited and people we saw. We can change it later if we want."

They flipped through their notepads and pressed sticky

notes onto the paper. When they stepped away, the makeshift crime board was divided into four columns: The Wyeth house, the historical society museum, Carriage House Antiques, and The Busy Bean. Each column contained sticky notes of who had been at each location.

"For now, I say we focus on the people we don't know." Ina uncapped a red marker. "The man we saw outside the historical society and Juliet." She put red stars beside their names.

"And Francesco, of course," Maggie added, circling his name in purple.

Ina pursed her lips and studied the board. "Oh, what about the other man Ruth said was at the museum asking about the circus before we arrived?"

"Oh yeah," Maggie said. She scribbled *First man to visit museum per Ruth* on a sticky note and posted it. "And I think we should add the motorcycle men. Francesco acted squirrelly when he saw them. And he spoke to them outside."

"Good idea."

Maggie added the sticky notes, then scanned the chart and recited the names of people and places they listed. "I know we weren't going to include friends, but the circus was mentioned by several people. The first time was at Hattie Wyeth's house."

Ina's face clouded. "I don't think Shelley—"

"I know, but humor me, please. The connection is slim, but it *is* a connection."

"How so?"

"Past or present, they were all somehow connected to the Circus de Vita."

"Okay." Ina stared at the board for several seconds while Maggie added Shelley's name to the chart. "Don't forget the blonde with the briefcase who walked by the crime scene."

Maggie added a sticky note for the briefcase woman. Biting

her lip, she slowly turned to face Ina, debating whether or not she should add one more sticky note.

"Spit it out," Ina said, hands on her hips. "Something else is on your mind. I can tell."

"There's something I didn't tell you yesterday."

"Well, do share."

"I think we were followed on the way to your house, but I believe I lost him before we turned onto your street." Maggie steeled herself for Ina's reaction.

"I know." A smile tugged at Ina's lips. "I saw it in the passenger side-view mirror. I told you I knew we weren't tailed by the time we got here."

Maggie shook her head and chuckled. *Not exactly the reaction I expected, but considering who it is, I should have.* "You don't miss a thing."

"You ought to know that about me by now." Ina grinned. "So, what's the next step?"

"We should find out more about Francesco."

"I knew we'd need this." Ina pulled a small piece of paper from her pants pocket and handed it to Maggie. "Here's the information from Francesco's business card. Why don't you try calling his work number and see who answers?"

"Worth a shot." Maggie sat down and pulled her cell phone from her purse. She dialed the number and listened to the phone ring four times.

"*New York Examiner,* Estella Flores here." The woman sounded a bit like Jennifer Lopez.

Maggie grabbed her pen and scratched the woman's name on her notepad and took a deep breath. "Ms. Flores, my name is Maggie Watson. I'm calling from Somerset Harbor, Maine."

"I'm sorry. You're calling from where?"

Maggie switched on her speakerphone so Ina could hear the

conversation. "Somerset Harbor, Maine. I met Francesco Valli here yesterday shortly before he died."

"Oh yeah?" The *clack* of fingers striking a keyboard indicated Estella was taking notes.

"I'm sorry for your loss." Maggie paused, choosing her words carefully. "I'm trying to make sense of what happened yesterday, and I'd like to ask you a few questions about Mr. Valli."

"With all due respect, Ms. Watson, usually the reporter is the one who asks the questions."

"I'm sorry." Maggie searched for the right words. "He seemed like such a nice guy. I'm trying to figure out why someone would want to kill him."

"Where did you meet him?"

"The place where he was mur—" She bit off the word. "We met at a café called The Busy Bean. He introduced himself and asked to join our table."

"What did Francesco say during your conversation?"

"He said he was writing a book about the entertainment industry. And he was particularly interested in the circus." Maggie didn't want to answer questions when she had so many of her own. "Why was he interested in this circus, and why Somerset Harbor?"

Estella Flores hesitated as if deciding whether or not to answer. "Evidently, Francesco believed a specific celebrity—and no, I don't know which one—had been in the circus years ago and his last show had been in your town."

Maggie tapped her pen on the table. "Did he contact anybody at the circus?"

"We don't know." The typing sounds stopped. "The paper will be following this story. Francesco was a respected journalist. We want to know what happened to him. If you find out anything, will you give me a call back?"

"I'd hardly be the first to know anything," Maggie said. "But I'll call if I hear something."

. . . .

The full moon was playing hide-and-seek behind scattered clouds when Maggie pulled the Jetta into the circular drive in front of Sedgwick Manor that evening. She leaned forward against the steering wheel and studied the eerie shadows shifting with the clouds.

Full moon, creepy clouds, and a dark house. Maggie shivered. *If this was in a horror flick, haunting music would be cueing the bad guy, and the heroine would be doing something stupid.*

Taking a deep breath, Maggie grabbed her purse and opened the door, opting to leave the antique quilt locked in the trunk for the night. She was tired and still unnerved about Francesco's murderer possibly lurking around town. Sewing could wait.

Maggie trudged up the walkway, her feet feeling like cinder blocks. All she wanted was to sip a cup of tea and sit in her favorite library chair with a purring Snickers on her lap. She was about to start up the steps to the door when a willowy figure moved from the shadows.

"I want to—" The soft, female voice stopped as a car approached. Seconds later, the lithe silhouette danced away and vanished in the shadows.

5

Her heart pounding like a jackhammer, Maggie stared into the shadows, hoping to glimpse a movement. But the only motion she saw was in her peripheral vision as she caught sight of the police car pulling up next to the curb. She considered her options: do nothing, chase the woman, or talk to the cops. *Who could she be? And why did her voice sound vaguely familiar?*

Clouds drifted in front of the moon like curtains closing. The woman had likely found a place to hide or made it to a waiting getaway vehicle and was on her way to being long gone. Maggie pulled her cell phone from her purse, switched on the flashlight app so the officers would see her, and hustled down the walkway. Officers Linton and Crosby got out of the car and met her on the sidewalk next to the cruiser.

"Everything okay, Mrs. Watson?"

Maggie was tempted to tell Officer Crosby to call her Maggie in light of how often she'd been called to Sedgwick Manor. "Everything is fine, I think. Haven't been in the house yet. I came home to a surprise visitor outside, and it was rather unnerving. She ran away when your car approached."

Officer Linton raised his eyebrows. "She? Can you describe her?"

"I couldn't see too well in the dark, but the voice sounded feminine. She didn't say enough for me to hear an accent."

Robert scratched his chin. "What happened, exactly?"

Maggie described leaving Ina's house, driving home, and finding the woman near the front door. "She sounded more mysterious than dangerous, but I believe she knows something about the murder."

The police officers exchanged looks. "I'm going to make a quick phone call," Officer Crosby said. She climbed into the cruiser.

Officer Linton returned his gaze to Maggie. "Did she threaten you?"

"She said, 'I want to,' then stopped. I think she was about to say more before she saw your car and bolted."

He stared at the house for several seconds, then looked back at the patrol car. "When Officer Crosby finishes her call, we'll make sure everything is clear in the house before we leave. Patrols will continue to roll by throughout the night."

Maggie managed to smile. "Thank you. I know I didn't truly witness the murder and Francesco was a stranger, but the whole thing has me on edge."

The car door slammed shut and Officer Crosby rejoined them. "All clear at Ina's place."

Officer Linton nodded. "Good. I'll walk the perimeter. You look inside."

As he cut through the yard to check the side of the house facing the antiques shop, Officer Crosby accompanied Maggie to the front door of the manor. The bushes on either side of the steps swayed in the breeze. Maggie inserted her key in the lock and turned it, then stepped out of the way so Officer Crosby could enter the foyer first.

The house was quiet and dark save for the night-light burning at the bottom of the curved staircase. Maggie flipped the light switch by the door and looked up as the crystal chandelier sparked to life. She turned sharply toward the kitchen when she heard a strange *smack* from that direction.

Officer Crosby removed her gun from its holster and signaled Maggie to remain in the foyer. The *ticktock* of the grandfather clock seemed louder than usual as the officer crept down the hallway toward the kitchen. Maggie held her breath as Officer Crosby disappeared.

A few seconds later, light emanated from the kitchen. "Maggie, you have a thief in here," the officer called.

"Is it safe for me to go in there?"

"Yes." The single word was filled with amusement.

Maggie strode down the hallway and stopped at the door with a gasp. "Snickers!"

The cat, one paw protecting a partially eaten steak, looked up with big eyes and meowed. His tail swished back and forth on the floor.

"You, Mr. Snickers, are lucky I'm crazy about you," Maggie said, hands on her hips, a smile tugging at her lips. "Otherwise, you'd be on your way out the door. I had that steak thawing on the counter for my dinner."

"Stay with the cat," Officer Crosby said. "I'll be back in a minute." She walked through the breakfast room and disappeared into the living room.

Maggie picked up the steak, put it in a sealable plastic bag, and marked it *for Snickers* with a permanent marker. "I'm not very hungry anyway," she said, tossing the package into the refrigerator. Maggie cleaned steak juice from the floor with a disinfectant wipe. After tossing the wipe in the garbage, she eyed Snickers. "I hope you enjoyed your steak dinner. If you behave, I'll cook the rest of it when things die down a bit. I'm too tired to do it tonight."

Maggie scooped up the cat and paced around the kitchen and breakfast room, waiting for the officers to reappear. She rubbed her cheek on the top of his head, thankful he was safe from shadowy interlopers. He purred and licked her nose with his rough tongue. "You stinker, you know I can't stay mad at you too long."

"All clear upstairs," Officer Crosby said, stepping into the kitchen at the same time her partner tapped on the side door to the sunroom. She followed Maggie to the door and peered out the window until Officer Linton gave a slight nod, then stepped aside. "It's okay. You can open the door."

With Snickers still cuddled in one arm, Maggie pulled the door open with her free hand.

"All quiet outside," Robert said, walking over the threshold. "Everything okay in here?"

"Yes." Officer Crosby smiled. "All we found was a partially eaten steak consumed by a hungry feline. He gave us a start when he pushed it off the counter, and it hit the floor with a thud. But the perpetrator has been subdued."

Officer Linton winked at Maggie, who still clutched Snickers. "A real cat burglar, huh?" His smile flickered and was gone. "All kidding aside, I didn't find anything outside, but that doesn't mean you can let your guard down. Call us if the woman or anyone else shows up uninvited."

Maggie nodded. "I'll call, I promise."

"We'll hold you to that," Officer Crosby said.

Maggie led the officers to the front door. "Your timing was perfect tonight. I'm thankful you arrived when you did."

"We are too," Robert said, opening the door.

Maggie smiled as she bid the officers good evening, but her smile faded as they descended her front steps and walked out into the darkness toward their squad car. She closed the door and locked it behind her.

· · · · · · · · · · · · · · · ·

"Now, hold still. You need a touch of extra color on your face." Juliet leaned toward Maggie, brandishing a makeup brush.

The bristles were soft and familiar but confusing. Maggie pushed her hand away, mumbling, "I can do it myself. I don't like much blush on my cheeks."

Juliet was relentless with the brush. The more Maggie pushed it away, the quicker it returned to her cheekbone. "Stop!" Maggie protested.

Juliet glared at her, but when she opened her mouth to speak, she roared like a lion.

Maggie woke with a start to find a wide-eyed Snickers on her stomach, his paw gingerly brushing her cheek. The cat's gentle meow brought her back to her senses. "Thank goodness it's you," she said, scratching him behind the ears. "I was in danger of looking like a clown if you hadn't woken me when you did."

She rubbed her eyes and shook her head. The novel she'd been reading was wedged between her hip and the sofa back. Her mug rested on the coffee table next to her cell phone. Maggie collected her thoughts. She'd slept fitfully and awakened long before daylight, her imagination conjuring intruders with every creak of the manor's old bones. Finally, she'd risen around six o'clock, taken a hot shower, and hunkered down in the living room to read.

Down the hall, the grandfather clock chimed ten times. *Ten already? I must have slept for a couple of hours.* Her cell phone rang just after the last stroke. Maggie moved Snickers, sat up, and answered her phone. "Good morning, June."

"Good morning to you too. The pieces from the Wyeth house have arrived. I'm dying to check them out. Want to come over?"

"That was fast."

June chuckled. "I bribed Bobby and his friend Jarrod with all the pizza and soda they could consume if they'd pick up the items yesterday afternoon. They jumped at the offer."

"You are a wise woman, June McGillis," Maggie said. "Robert and Nora sure have raised their son right. Anyway, I'd love the distraction from thinking about the murder. Give me an hour to freshen up, and I'll head your way."

· · · · · · · · · · · · · · · · ·

Maggie walked into the receiving area of Carriage House Antiques and found her shop manager staring into the top of Hattie Wyeth's Victorian aquarium.

"What in the world?" June muttered. She scratched her head as she examined the aquarium's contents: a pint-size fantasy world comprising fairies, dragons, and even a miniature castle.

Standing in the doorway, Maggie laughed. "Problem?"

"Oh, good morning." June startled, her eyes widened. "I didn't hear you come in."

"I know you didn't. You were too busy exploring Dragon Land."

"I heard Hattie Wyeth was quite the eccentric in her later years, but I didn't expect to find a fantasy-themed terrarium inside a Victorian aquarium most likely created to hold goldfish."

"To be fair, it matches the base." Maggie walked around the aquarium and studied the trio of winged dragons circling the heavy, ornate stand. "Looks like it belongs in a fairy-tale castle or something."

"I've never seen anything like it. For better or worse." June grinned, then turned to the game chair and traced her fingertips across the three carved arcs across the back. "Now this is what I call a cool piece."

"It is." Maggie smiled, Ina's demonstration of the chair's secret places playing through her mind. "You should have heard Ina reminiscing about her childhood visits to the Wyeth house. She was almost giddy while telling me about this chair."

"I can imagine. Hattie and Ina were buddies since grade school. Lots of memories."

"Lots of secrets too, I bet." Maggie sat on one of the three leather cushions on the conversation settee as June explored the chair's hidden compartments. "I bet Hattie knew why Ina doesn't drive. Do you?"

"I have no idea. I've never asked, and Ina's never said."

"Well, I asked as we were leaving the Wyeth house."

"Aren't you the brave one?" June knelt on the floor in front of the chair and ran her hands along the carved vine and flowers. "What'd she say?"

"All she said was, 'I just don't.' And then she made it clear she didn't want to talk about it." Maggie shrugged. "I don't get it."

"Me either. Just doesn't match her adventurous personality. After all, she climbed Mount Katahdin when she was in her fifties." June leaned closer to the chair and squealed with delight when she opened the drawer under the seat. She raised her head, strawberry-blonde bangs falling over her eyebrows, and grinned. "Maggie, there's a carved chessboard in here. It's gorgeous."

"Really?" Maggie rose from the settee and peered into the chessboard drawer. "I didn't notice it when Ina opened that drawer the other day."

"Let's take a closer look." June pulled the drawer out farther and eased the chessboard from the compartment. "Wow, the board is remarkably heavy." Holding the chessboard on her lap with one hand, she reached into the drawer with the other. "There's something in the back corner. Here, take the board."

Maggie sat on the floor, tucked her knees under her, and slid the chessboard onto her lap.

June thrust her arm into the drawer. "It's a huge ring," she said, pulling out an oversize metal signet ring and holding it in the air for examination. "It says 'Big Jake the Giant' on the top. The name 'Circus de Vita' is etched on the inside."

"A giant's ring." Maggie held out her hand and June passed her the ring. "How remarkable."

"You never know what we'll find tucked inside antiques, huh? These were popular souvenirs back in the early and mid-1900s."

Maggie held the ring in the palm of her hand. "This would fit around a child's wrist. I'll bet Hattie got it at the circus when she was a girl. Maybe even when she went with Ina."

"You're probably right. I think we should give it to Ina. She might like it to go with the other stuff Hattie left her."

Maggie pictured Ina's odd reaction to the circus memorabilia in the box at the Wyeth house. "Maybe." Her cell phone rang before she could say more. She passed the ring and chessboard to June and plucked her cell phone from her pocket. "It's Shelley Wyeth Mooreland. Wonder what she wants."

June shrugged, and Maggie answered the call.

"Maggie, I found something you might be interested in while cleaning out Mom's storage room." Shelley's voice sounded tired. "It's a large framed circus poster. The design is different, I think, from the one she left for Ina in the box. Would you like to come see it this afternoon?"

"This is a good time to sell circus memorabilia with everyone so excited about the upcoming shows by Circus de Vita." Maggie eyed the giant's ring in June's hand. "Would sometime between one and two o'clock work for you?"

"Perfect. I'll see you then."

Maggie ended the call and told June about the framed poster. "I think it's worth a look."

"Definitely." June returned the chessboard and the ring to the chair's drawer, then stepped back and studied the other pieces from the Wyeth house. She checked her watch. "Why don't we snap photos of a few of these new items? We can collage them with images of our fall displays in the flyer I started. If we hurry, it can be ready for you to drop by the printshop after checking out the circus poster."

"Sure thing. Then we can finish up the fall displays we started the other day and you can get photos of those too."

Maggie and June chatted as they took the photos, then migrated to the sales floor to work on the vignettes.

"You know, I wasn't so sure when you bought this thing,"

Maggie said, looking down from a stepladder while arranging a garland of dried maple leaves across the top of a massive primitive cupboard. "But I've come to appreciate how the old white paint shows through the chipped green layer. She has character."

June emptied a coffee can full of acorns into an old pottery bowl decorated with a brown, blue, and green floral pattern. "I knew you'd see what makes her special. It'll take just the right buyer to appreciate her character, but one will come along."

Maggie climbed down the stepladder and brushed the palms of her hands on her slacks. "Is it weird that I almost don't want it to sell?"

"Happens to all of us. We find that one piece we don't want to turn loose." June chuckled and placed the bowl of acorns between two carved-wood candlesticks in the center of a white pine table. "I'm sort of fond of the old beast myself."

"So I'm not weird after all?"

"Now, I didn't say that," June teased. "Be right back. I'm going to get my camera."

Maggie strolled through the shop, pleased with the current inventory and seasonal decorations. She took a few moments to appreciate the business she'd learned and the friends she'd made since moving to Somerset Harbor.

"I love this camera. It's an oldie but a goody," June said, returning with a hefty black professional-grade camera that required two hands to operate. She drew closer to the green cupboard and snapped a few photos. "It's an older digital. Got it used for a steal at the camera shop several years ago. Some freelance photojournalist traded it in while he was in town working on a travel piece for a magazine. He even threw in a zoom lens."

"It may be old for a digital camera, but it's a lot younger than Ina's box camera." Maggie joined June as she moved around the shop taking photos of the newly completed displays. She imagined

Ina using her clunky box camera for the same task. "June, did you know Ina was a photographer in her youth?"

June paused, holding her camera waist high between her hands. "I remember seeing a few old newspapers with some of her photos in them. Really old papers. I think Ina was in high school at the time."

"She's a woman of many talents, isn't she? I had no idea Ina had been into photography until Shelley Wyeth gave her the box from Hattie."

"I think Ina has pretty much been a free spirit her entire life." June led Maggie toward the office. "She never had a man to tie her down, so she dabbled in whatever struck her fancy. Pretty cool, if you ask me."

"I agree," Maggie said, pulling a chair up to the computer. "I've known her for a while now, but since we witnessed the murder, I feel like I'm only beginning to get a glimpse of who she is. Do you have any idea why she never married?"

"Never found the right man, I guess." June focused her attention on uploading the new photos from the camera to the computer. When the images were finished transferring, she opened the file for the flyer she'd created earlier and began rearranging copy and dropping photos into it. "I guess everybody has secrets." She moved a photo of the game chair closer to the bottom of the page. "We never know when or how they'll be revealed."

6

The poster Shelley had called about was stunning, and Maggie found herself mesmerized by the glimpse it offered into circus history. Deep primary colors brought the artwork's vivid details to life. A sleek black frame, glossy but plain, didn't dare steal any attention away from the poster's dramatic flair.

"I'm sorry I didn't offer this when you were here the other day," Shelley said. "I didn't find it until this morning, when my husband and I were going through my mother's closet. The poster was hidden in the very back." She blinked back tears. "I've been putting off going through her closet. It's so hard."

Maggie nodded, remembering the pain she experienced after her own mother's death. "It's in perfect condition for a piece tucked away for who knows how long."

Shelley dabbed her eyes with a tissue. "I was happy to find a couple of old family portraits back there too. I'm taking those back to Portland with me."

Shelley had removed the portrait of her grandfather from over the parlor fireplace and replaced it with the circus poster so Maggie could see it to best effect beneath an overhead light. The light illuminated more detail than Maggie had expected. Designed to highlight the circus headliners, the poster featured a ringmaster in top hat and tails with his cane raised. A golden-haired dancer stood in an arabesque on the back of a white stallion leading a line of four brown horses around a ring. Just outside the bottom of the ring, a strongman hefted a barbell, and a juggler kept four red spheres in the air above his head. Two spotlights shone down from the right corner. One featured a handsome tightrope walker, and the other, a pair of trapeze artists. A large, grinning clown face gazed down from the opposite corner. *Circus de Vita* was emblazoned in bright red across the top in a chunky, whimsical font. Along the bottom, black lettering heralded, *Somerset Harbor, September 13-16.*

"Do you mind if I take a quick photo and text it to my shop manager?" Maggie pulled her phone from her pocket as she asked.

"Go right ahead."

Maggie pulled her phone from her purse, snapped a photo, and texted it to June along with a short note: *The poster is gorgeous. Will have it in the shop this afternoon.*

Maggie tried to picture a young Ina memorializing her trips to the circus with her camera. "Shelley, was your mother a big fan of the circus?"

"A huge fan." Shelley flicked a speck of dust off the frame. "Mom always said she tagged along with the Lintons whenever they went to the circus. One year when she was around thirteen, Mom had the flu and couldn't go. She'd made Ina promise to bring back souvenirs for her. She fulfilled her promise, but Mom said Ina never attended the circus again."

"Any idea why?"

"None at all. Mom always seemed bewildered by it."

"Huh." Maggie took a few paces backward and looked up. "Anyway, I'd like this poster. How much do you want for it?"

The two women negotiated the price easily. In the end, Maggie was pleased with the deal she'd made. She declined Shelley's offer to have her husband drop the poster by the shop the following day and opted to take it with her. "Thanks for giving me first dibs," she said, watching Shelley lift it from the wall and climb down the stepladder.

"Of course," Shelley said. "Mom would have wanted it that way."

While Shelley wrapped the frame in an old towel, Maggie's phone chimed with an incoming text from June. *Poster is fantastic! Can't wait to see it in person.*

Shelley escorted Maggie to the door and followed her to the car. "Let me know if you're able to get Ina to say why she wouldn't go back to the circus. Mom always wondered."

So, even Ina's best friend didn't know why she was weird about the circus. Balancing the poster against her hip with one arm, Maggie pulled her car keys from her purse with the opposite hand and unlocked the door. "Don't hold your breath, but I'll let you know if she mentions it."

"Thanks. I'd really like to know. It would be like solving a mystery for Mom."

Maggie lowered the poster into the trunk of her car. "I'd like to solve that one myself."

. . . .

"'Chuppta?" Stan Marlowe asked as Maggie crossed the planked floor of The Village Printshop. "Time for the annual fall sale flyer?"

Maggie smiled at Stan's two-syllable way of asking what she was up to. Born and raised in Somerset Harbor, his vocabulary was full of Mainer expressions. Maggie showed him a file folder. "How did you know?"

"You keep the exact same schedule as your aunt Evelyn, and that's a good thing," he said, pulling his reading glasses from his shirt pocket and placing them atop his bulbous nose. "Let's see what you have there."

"We e-mailed you the file a little while ago, but I thought I'd stop by anyway." Maggie slid the folder in the widest space between several bundled stacks of papers lining the counter. Inside was a printout of the flyer June had made with a few notes about quantity and paper type on top. "How soon can you get this ready?"

"Probably won't get to it until tomorrow. Everyone has some sort of seasonal event happening these days." He pulled the folder toward him and opened it. "Very eye-catching."

"I'll tell June you said so. She's a whiz with computer graphics."

"That she is, and you've developed quite an eye for antiques," he said, pulling an order form from a shelf behind the counter and transferring over the order information from the printout.

Maggie felt a swell of pride at his compliment. "You're too kind."

"Just telling the truth as I see it." Stan scribbled on the order form and turned it to face Maggie. "Sign the bottom, and we're all set."

She skimmed the form, signed it, and pushed it back across the counter.

Stan clipped the flyer and work order together and tossed them into a wooden box. "I'll call the shop when they're ready."

"We'll be waiting." Maggie waved goodbye and headed toward the door.

Mentally checking the flyers off her to-do list, Maggie stepped onto the sidewalk to find the sun had disappeared and the wind had whipped up during her few minutes inside the printshop. She brushed her windblown hair from her eyes and started toward her car. After two paces, she stopped dead in her tracks. Juliet stood at the corner in animated conversation with a broad-shouldered, sandy-haired man Maggie didn't recognize. Continuing toward her car, Maggie smiled and nodded as a frowning Juliet, whose hair miraculously remained perfectly coiffed in the wind, looked up and pointed in her direction.

Relieved to reach her car, Maggie slid behind the wheel and took a couple of deep breaths. *I don't even want to know why Juliet is pointing me out.* She backed her car into the street and put it into gear. As she turned the wheel, a movement across the street caught her eye. She inched forward as a woman stood up from a bench, newspaper in hand, and looked straight at her.

Maggie locked eyes with the blonde woman she'd seen leaving the murder scene. The mystery woman had exchanged her business suit and heels for green athletic tights and a pair of trail-running shoes.

Maggie snatched her cell phone from the seat beside her and tried to snap a photo as the woman turned and dashed in the opposite direction, but her quarry was too quick. Not wanting to let the woman get away, she quickly dropped her phone onto the passenger seat, threw her gear shift into drive, and spun her steering wheel to whip into a parking space across the street. In a flash, she grabbed her phone and keys with one hand while flinging her door open with the other.

By the time Maggie reached the sidewalk, the blonde was halfway down the block, leaving a line of startled onlookers gaping after her. Maggie gave thanks for her choice of sensible shoes as she sprinted down the street toward The Busy Bean. She groaned a minute later when the woman vanished.

Maggie paused to catch her breath, taking in deep gulps of air as frustration riveted through her. *Where'd she go?* The blonde was nowhere in sight, but most of the pedestrians were staring down an alley between two shops.

"Excuse me," Maggie said, brushing against shoulders as she made her way to the alley opening. It had rained the night before, and mud puddles and scattered debris—including damp cardboard boxes, empty paint-spattered cans, and drenched newspapers—remained in the paved canyon between the rows of old buildings. Clutching her phone more tightly than usual, Maggie took tentative steps into the alley as the crowd began to dissipate. Water from an earlier rainstorm dripped from gutters and rooftops. Music filtered through an open window. A chubby cat walked along the edge of a Dumpster.

But she saw no sign of the blonde woman or anyone else.

Maggie shoved her phone into the back pocket of her jeans. An undercurrent of panic coursed through her when she realized she'd left her pepper spray in the car with her purse. Her mind scrambled for an answer. Her keys. Maggie held her key ring with two keys sticking out between the three middle fingers of her right hand. It wasn't much of a defense, but at least it was something.

Heart pounding, she moved down the alley with slow, deliberate steps. A loud *bang* reverberated through the alley as a glass jug skipped down a pile of trash and bounced off the Dumpster. Turning toward the sound, her keyed fist raised, she found the cat at the top of the garbage pile, peering down at her. She let out a breath she hadn't realized she'd been holding.

When she regained her wits, Maggie continued down the alley with larger steps. The cat continued to knock objects onto the pavement. "It's a cat," Maggie muttered. "Nothing to worry about. The mystery woman must be a mile away by now."

A distinctly human grunt sounded from halfway down the alley. Maggie was shocked to find a metal garbage can hurtling toward her. Dropping her keys, she spun out of the way fast enough to keep the can from grazing her shoulder. Losing her balance, Maggie fell to the ground. She nearly growled in disappointment as the blonde sprinted out of the alley.

The can rolled until it hit a wall of crates stacked along a building. Maggie glanced up and down the alley. It was deserted. The woman had created a diversion long enough to get Maggie off her trail.

Maggie fished her keys out of a dirty puddle. She rose to her knees and pulled the cell phone from her pocket to make sure it hadn't broken when she fell. She sighed in relief when the screen lit up. She rose to her feet and took stock of her surroundings. She was alone in the quiet alley.

7

By the time Maggie arrived at her car, her heart rate was normal and she was convinced the trash can had been thrown more as a diversion than a weapon. Climbing into the driver's seat, she dialed Ina's number.

Ina picked up on the first ring. "Maggie. Everything okay?"

"I saw the strangest things when I came out of the printshop, and I think they could be important."

"Tell me."

Ina was quiet while Maggie described nearly bumping into Juliet. "Ina, she glared at me while pointing me out to some strange guy. It was weird."

"Sure sounds like it. That woman gave me the creeps. And her flirting with James is shameful."

Maggie didn't want to think about James and Juliet. "There's more."

"Sheesh, what else did she do?"

"Nothing that I know of." Maggie thought back to the blonde woman. She was certain this was the woman carrying the briefcase to the SUV after the murder. "Right after I ran into Juliet, I saw the blonde who walked by right after Francesco was killed. She was across the street from the printshop."

"I'll add it to our crime board." Ina's voice was laced with excitement. "We'll solve this murder yet."

"I hope so." Maggie smiled at Ina's enthusiasm. "I'm going to give Robert a call and fill him in just in case we're onto something here." She paused, then said, "I also wanted to tell you about the circus poster I picked up from Shelley this afternoon. It's stunning."

"Oh, my pot's boiling over. You'll have to tell me another time. Give my love to Robert, please." Ina signed off before Maggie could say another word.

"Well, goodbye to you too." Unnerved by Ina's reaction, Maggie dialed Robert's cell number. After the fourth ring, his voice mail picked up. Frustrated, Maggie sighed and ended the call without leaving a message.

She started the car and pulled away from the curb. Restless after Ina's abrupt ending to their phone call, Maggie stopped by the library to check out a book on circus history, pulled into the gas station to fill up her car, and ran into the market to pick up a few staple items before heading home.

Back at the manor, her cell phone rang just as she finished putting away her groceries.

"Emily, what a lovely surprise," Maggie said, closing the pantry door. Phone calls from her daughter, who lived a few hours away in Boston, were Maggie's favorite kind of interruption.

"I just got off my shift and you were on my mind, so I thought I'd call."

"I'm glad you did," Maggie said, taking a seat at the breakfast table.

"Mom, you sound tired. What's wrong?"

"Everything's fine, honey." Maggie didn't want Emily to worry. "I've had a busy day. I picked up a gorgeous 1950s circus poster for a steal. It belonged to a childhood friend of Ina's."

"Sounds cool."

"June and I think there'll be good interest in it around here. The circus is rolling into town this week." Maggie gazed out the window at the colorful fall foliage rustling in a late-afternoon breeze. "How's Austin?"

"He's wonderful." Emily's voice had a dreamlike quality

when she talked about her boyfriend. "But he's working late tonight, so I'm on my own for dinner."

"Must be tough finding time to spend with each other with careers keeping you busy."

"Yeah, but it's worth it." Emily's voice was full of happiness. "If the weather clears, we're going to hike Wachusett Mountain next week. Miracle of miracles, we're scheduled to have the same days off."

Maggie's heart swelled. Emily was in love with a fine young man. Emily had brought Dr. Austin Prescott, an orthopedic doctor at Boston's Brigham and Women's Hospital, home to meet her during the summer, and Maggie instantly liked the affable, bright young doctor who was obviously head over heels for her daughter.

"And your job?"

"Oh Mom, I can't describe how much I love being a nurse at Massachusetts General. The hours are long and the work is demanding, but helping these babies and their families through difficult situations is more rewarding than I can say." She finally paused for a breath. "You're awfully quiet. Are you sure everything is all right? Is Snickers okay?"

"Snickers is more than okay." Maggie chuckled. "Last night he had a steak dinner on me."

"Now I know something's up. Although he's adorable, I can't imagine you cooking Snickers a steak dinner."

"Well, I didn't exactly cook him a steak dinner." Maggie soon had Emily laughing as she described Snickers as a beef thief she'd mistaken for a burglar. She was surprised to find herself laughing along. Emily's phone calls were balm for her soul.

Maggie heard a break in the connection indicating Emily had an incoming call.

"Mom, I gotta go. Austin's calling. Hopefully he's letting me know we'll be able to have dinner together after all."

"Thanks for calling. I love you."

After she ended the call, Maggie sat for a minute with her eyes closed, Emily's "Love you too" echoing through her mind. A sense of peace engulfed her. She basked in it for a few minutes, then figured she ought to head over to the shop to show June the poster.

The framed poster was still in her trunk, so she drove over to the shop instead of walking the path through the woods. As she approached Carriage House Antiques, she noticed that James's Mercedes was parked in the lot. She pulled into the space beside his car. Leaving the poster in her trunk, Maggie walked to the shop door. As she reached for the handle, the door opened from the inside.

"Don't look so shocked." James grinned from the doorway. "I was watching through the window when you drove in. June said she was expecting you to arrive any time with a large framed poster. Want some help?"

"That'd be nice. Thanks." Maggie glanced through the doorway to see if Juliet was lurking behind him. She was relieved to spot neither the perfectly coiffed hair nor the flawlessly manicured fingernails of the designer.

Halfway to the car, James stopped and placed his hand on her arm. "June told me what happened when you arrived home last night." He looked down at her, his eyes serious. "I'm worried about you."

"Last night was spooky, but I'm fine. The police are watching the shop and the manor."

"And you?"

Maggie smiled. "I have a hunch they're keeping an eye on me too."

"Maggie, if you've witnessed a murder, you need a security system. At the very least, please consider having one installed in the house."

"Now that's an interesting comment coming from someone who doesn't even have a password on his cell phone," Maggie teased, attempting to lighten the conversation. She pointed her key fob at the Jetta and hit the button to unlock the doors. "The poster's in the trunk."

"Oh, there you are." Juliet's high-pitched voice whistled across the parking lot from the direction of the shop. "What are you doing out here?"

James opened the trunk door. "I'm helping Maggie carry this framed poster." He lifted the towel-wrapped poster out carefully.

"Oh. Well, come inside. I found a gorgeous piece for the Witmarsh place." Juliet stood in the doorway, her hands on her hips.

"Heading that way."

Maggie whistled and said under her breath, "Are all high-powered interior designers so impatient?"

James chuckled. "She can be a little intense."

Juliet moved out of the doorway as Maggie followed James, who carried the bulky poster inside the building.

"Where do you want it?" he asked.

"I have an easel waiting over here. Follow me," June said, motioning him to an ornate easel nestled among two potted plants and three large carved animals: a tiger, lion, and elephant.

James let the towel fall from the frame to the floor and lowered the poster onto the easel. He stepped back a few paces. "It is rather striking, isn't it?"

"Why are people in this town so obsessed with the circus?" Juliet pulled James out of the way, crossed her arms, and stared at the display.

"Many of us have fond memories of attending the circus with our parents," James said. "Years ago, people in my mother's generation had to go to Portland to experience anything other than local entertainment. The annual arrival of the circus was an exciting time. I'll admit I felt a thrill when I saw the circus trucks rolling into town earlier today, even though I haven't been to a show in years."

Without saying a word, Juliet bent over and repositioned the potted plants in front of the easel. She then nestled the carved animals among the plants. "There, that's better," she said, standing up and wiping her hands together as if brushing dust off them.

June's elbow dug into Maggie's side. Maggie willed her friend to remain professional, although she wanted to throttle the woman herself. Juliet's healthy self-confidence and condescending attitude rubbed her the wrong way, to say the least. But Maggie managed a smile. "Nice touch, Juliet."

"My career revolves around my superb eye for detail." Juliet's smile was a bit too exaggerated. "Although circus memorabilia isn't my thing."

"I will say, the poster is eye-catching." James leaned in for a closer look. "The dates don't include the year. What's your guess?"

"Mid- to late '50s, I suppose," June said.

Juliet rolled her eyes and sighed. "Why are we still talking about the circus?"

"You're right," June said. "Let's take another look at the statuary pieces you were interested in when you visited the first time." June glanced over her shoulder and winked at Maggie as she led Juliet to the back of the shop.

"Good idea," Maggie said. She pulled out her cell phone and snapped a photo of the display, then stepped forward and took a close-up of the poster. "With all the conversation about the circus, I'm likely to be asked for a photo of the poster while I'm out and about."

James watched June and Juliet meander among displays of furniture. When they disappeared, he placed his hand on her forearm. "Maggie, do you have time to meet for lunch tomorrow?

I've been tied up with the Witmarsh restoration and haven't had a chance to catch up with you."

"Won't Juliet—"

He squeezed her arm. "She'll be lunching with Mrs. Witmarsh in hopes she can get hired to redecorate the family's Florida estate. Trust me, I'd rather have lunch with you."

"In that case, I'd love to. Where did you have in mind?"

"I thought we could try The Beacon. I haven't been there yet."

"The new restaurant in the old rope factory?"

"That's the one. I hear the food is fantastic." James pulled his cell phone from his back pocket and opened his calendar. "About one o'clock?"

"It's a date." Maggie blushed. "I mean, I'll see you there."

James finished entering the lunch date on his phone. "I look forward to it," he said, returning the phone to his pocket. "I guess we should go check on Juliet and June."

"I was about to suggest the same thing," Maggie said. "I don't think June was too amused when Juliet rearranged her display."

"Juliet can be difficult to take sometimes. She's especially competitive with other women."

Considering her impression of the designer, Maggie was surprised to find Juliet listening without interruption as June told her the history of a pair of sleek stone statues—a mermaid and merman. Maggie already knew the legend of the pair and its local history, but she enjoyed hearing the embellished version June was sharing with Juliet.

"Because mermaids are timeless, I think the statues would help bridge the gap between the new modern outdoor kitchen area and the formal gardens," June said, a hand on each statue.

"You might be right." Juliet walked from the mermaid to the merman. "I'd like to take a couple of photos and show them to my clients."

"Take as many as you like." June was in professional mode. "I need to have Maggie sign some paperwork, so we'll be just inside the office if you need us."

"Would you please take a picture of us with the statues first?" Not waiting for a reply, Juliet handed June her cell phone and pulled James closer to the mermaid. "Make sure you smile, darling."

A little dumbfounded, Maggie watched as Juliet positioned James exactly where she wanted him.

Juliet turned around, wrapped her arms around James, and leaned her head on his shoulder. "Say, 'Happy clients.'"

James didn't repeat the phrase, but he did smile.

The camera flashed while Juliet's mouth was open. June held out the phone to Juliet. "Perfect. Here you go. We need to take care of that paperwork. You two have fun." As soon as Juliet took the phone, June pushed Maggie toward the office.

"'Make sure you smile, darling,'" June said, imitating Juliet's delivery when they were in the office and safely out of earshot. "That woman would be so annoying if she hadn't just put two of the most expensive Wyeth pieces on hold."

"Really? Which two?" Maggie sank into the closest chair.

"The game chair and the library steps." June sat down in the chair next to her.

"Very nice." Maggie thought back to the afternoon they'd met Juliet. She'd been going on and on about the art nouveau pieces. Had it only been the day before yesterday? "She was super interested in the art nouveau display. Suppose there's any chance of selling her any of those pieces for her client with the quirky loft in New York City?"

"It depends, I guess, on whether or not it matters that she likes us in order to buy from us." June shrugged. "Juliet and I didn't get off to a very good start, and she acts like she's afraid you'll snatch James from her clutches."

"I can't imagine her being afraid of anything." Maggie sat in the desk chair and closed her eyes in concentration for a few seconds. "James said she's very competitive, especially with women. She might be more motivated if we had someone else showing interest in the pieces. Too bad we don't."

"Yeah, that would be nice," June said, rifling through a desk drawer. She smiled a little as she withdrew a sheet of paper with a short list of names on it. "Maybe I can come up with something."

"Such as?"

"This is a list of people who have looked at the art nouveau display. I think I'll make a few calls and see if any of them still happen to be interested." June inclined her head toward the door. "Why don't you go out and check on them?"

"No monkey business, right?"

"Absolutely not." June smiled a bit too sweetly. "I'm going to stir up a bit of competition. Entirely aboveboard."

With a short wave, Maggie left the office and returned to the sales floor. She found James and Juliet standing shoulder to shoulder in front of the primitive green cabinet and adjacent dining table display.

"Who in the world would ever want to buy that awful monstrosity?" Juliet grimaced and moved the bowl of acorns on the table over two inches. "Look, the paint is even chipped, so the old white layer shows."

Maggie moved the bowl back to its original spot. "It has character. It once belonged to Mrs. Avery, a widow who ran a boardinghouse here near the end of the nineteenth century. She was famous for cooking her special soup for any family experiencing illness."

"Isn't that sweet?" Juliet pulled her cell phone from her purse and scrolled through her messages, stopping to reply to a few of them.

"Maggie, good news." June materialized seemingly out of nowhere. "Bette Mathis said she's interested in several of the art nouveau pieces, particularly the hand-carved settee with the curved vine frame. She'll be over first thing in the morning to look at them again."

"Really? That could be the fastest turnaround yet." Maggie searched June's face. Her glee was sincere. "We put the display up late last week. I didn't expect pieces to sell so quickly."

"I guess I'd best take another peek at it." Juliet slid her phone into her purse. "Maybe I can come up with a better offer."

Maggie covered her mouth with a hand to disguise her involuntary smile as a yawn. "Excuse me. I didn't sleep well last night."

"Maggie, you've had a crazy week." June's eyes softened. "Why don't you head home, and I'll help Juliet? In addition to the art nouveau pieces, she wants to show James the carved rosewood armchair for the Witmarsh place. I can take care of it. Go."

Genuine fatigue washed over Maggie. "Thank you. I'll take you up on that offer. I need to catch up on sleep." She turned to Juliet and James, her eyes meeting his. "I'll see you soon."

Maggie grabbed her purse from the office and was halfway to the door when rain began pelting the roof of the shop. She plucked a blue umbrella from the antique majolica umbrella stand by the door. Watching from the open doorway as rain puddled in the parking lot, she peered at her Jetta parked beside James's Mercedes. Should she drive her car around to the front of the manor or scurry across the path to the side door?

She opened the umbrella, stepped into the parking lot, and looked toward the road. A patrol car slowed down and rolled past. Police sightings were becoming common outside Sedgwick Manor. At first they had unnerved her, but she was beginning to appreciate their presence.

Deciding that a little fresh, if wet, air would do her good, Maggie inhaled the clean scent of the rain and crossed the asphalt to the path leading home. Thanks to her weariness, the trek to the house felt a bit longer and more cumbersome than usual, but at least the rain had slacked a bit as Maggie approached the side door.

She felt relief as she pulled the key from her purse and unlocked one side of the French door. She pushed it open, stepped over the threshold, and froze inside the breakfast room. A muffled creaking came from nearby. *Is that sound the back door opening?* "Of course not," she muttered to herself. "The police are outside. You're imagining things."

After locking the side door behind her, Maggie breathed deeply and entered the shadowy kitchen. Three paces in, she spied envelopes strewn across the floor in front of the small desk where she'd stacked the mail before heading to the shop. She stood motionless, listening to the familiar muffled creaking of the old house. She held her breath, straining to hear any noise that didn't belong.

And then she heard it—the unmistakable sound of the back door closing and clicking into place.

8

Heart pounding so hard she felt it in her ears, Maggie flipped on the kitchen light and walked through the breakfast room. She tugged on the back door. As she expected, it opened without protest. Neither the deadlock nor knob lock was engaged. That was odd, because the recent increase in suspicious activity had motivated Maggie to double-check the locks when entering and leaving the house. She was positive all the doors were locked when she left today. The hair on her arms stood on end as she secured both locks with a firm *click*.

Her footsteps tapping on the hardwood floor, Maggie walked through the house, turning on lights as she went. In her bedroom, she found her dresser drawers not quite closed and her closet door ajar. The lid to her jewelry box was also open, yet it appeared nothing had been taken.

Maggie traipsed through the foyer. The grandfather clock's *ticktock* echoed down the hallway. Snickers was nowhere to be seen. Too unnerved to disturb the silence by calling his name, she flipped the switch to illuminate the chandelier and then turned toward the library, one of his favorite hiding places. A spine-chilling yowl pierced the air as Snickers flew down the stairs behind her, his ears back and his tail puffed up and twitching.

"Snickers." When the cat skidded to a stop by her feet, Maggie scooped him up and ran outside, murmuring his name and praying the police cruiser was still close. Clutching the petrified cat, she ran down the driveway and, once again, found Officers Linton and Crosby striding up to meet her in the waning daylight.

"Thank goodness you're here." Maggie came to a stop in front of the officers. "Did you see anyone out here, near the house?"

"Only a die-hard jogger trekking through the puddles." Officer Linton frowned. "Why?"

"Because when I came home from the shop, I heard someone slip out the back as I walked in the side door of the manor."

Officer Crosby frowned. "How long ago?"

"Only long enough for me to walk through the house and find mail scattered on the floor and drawers open. When I went by the staircase, Snickers came down them practically airborne, his fur standing on end." Maggie took a breath. "I didn't dare go upstairs."

"I'll go look for the jogger. Her red hair will be hard to miss." Officer Crosby turned on her heel and strode to the car.

The rain had slowed, but Officer Linton's hair was damp from the downpour. Rain beaded on his forehead. "Are you hurt?"

Maggie shook her head. "Spooked, but I'm okay."

"Tell me what happened, Maggie."

Thunder rumbled in the distance and Snickers, recuperated from the excitement of the intruder, struggled in Maggie's arms. "Can we go inside first? I don't want to put Snickers down outside with a killer on the loose."

"Sure. It sounds like we're in for more rain. I imagine Snickers would be even less pleased if he got caught in a deluge."

As they strolled to the house, Maggie described what happened from the time she left the shop to the moment she ran outside with Snickers. After they had entered the foyer, Officer Linton jotted down a few notes. "Let's retrace your steps starting at the side door. Have you moved anything since you came in?"

"No, except I did lock the back door."

They walked through the kitchen, breakfast room, and Maggie's sitting room and bedroom, Robert taking notes as they progressed through the house. "Did you check the dining room, library, and office?"

"I didn't have a chance. I was on my way to the library when Snickers came down the stairs glaring like a maniac. It was unlike him, so I grabbed him and bolted out the door."

Officer Linton raised his eyebrows. "You should have done that the second you heard the back door close."

"I couldn't do that. I had to check on Snickers."

"I see."

Another wave of rain pounded on the roof as they crossed the house to the dining room, feeling to Maggie like a harbinger of doom. Officer Linton opened the silverware drawer in the sideboard. "Your silver is untouched, like your jewelry. It looks like they were searching for something in particular instead of things to hock. Any idea what it could be?"

"None whatsoever. I'm an open book. I have no secrets except the name of the guy I crushed on in sixth grade. Hardly information worth breaking and entering."

Officer Linton's lips turned up briefly at this bit of personal information. "Let's check the library."

Maggie led him across the foyer into the library. Robert stepped to the center of the room. He locked eyes on Captain Sedgwick's portrait for a moment before pacing the perimeter of the room. "Anything out of place?"

She stared at the bookcase. "Weird."

"What's weird?"

"The library ladder is in a different position."

"Where was it before?"

Maggie walked to the center of the bookcase. "Here, in front of the poetry books. Before my life became embroiled in the murder of Francesco Valli, I read a magazine article about an artist who created paintings based on Samuel Taylor Coleridge's

'The Rime of the Ancient Mariner,' and I was researching more about the poem and the writer."

Officer Linton's head tilted back as he studied the bookcase. "There's a book missing."

"That's where the volume of poems by Romance-era poets was." She pointed to the tobacco stand by her favorite chair. "That's it on the tobacco stand. The library ladder has been moved, but I don't see where anything else was touched."

He eyed the tobacco stand. "The door isn't closed all the way."

Maggie inched closer and bent down to look. "You're right. It isn't, but there's nothing in it except for a collection of bookmarks, a few pens, and a package of highlighters."

Officer Linton used his pen to open the door to the stand. The contents were as Maggie listed, but they were piled on top of each other in one big heap. "Is this the way you usually keep these things organized?"

She peered into the small cabinet. "That kind of disorder drives me nuts. Someone has rummaged through it, but nothing is missing."

"Your office is next." Officer Linton went through the door leading into the room Maggie still often thought of as Aunt Evelyn's office.

"Oh no," Maggie groaned when she walked up beside him. "They weren't so careful in here."

The mahogany desk Maggie always kept so neat was in total disarray. Drawers gaped open, their contents strewn on the floor. Papers once nestled in the two-tier organizer were in a jumble on the desktop. The old-school phone receiver was off the hook, and the monotonous dial tone pierced the silence.

"They were looking for something specific," Officer Linton said, stepping in paperless patches of the floor as if crossing a river on rocks. "Any idea what it might be? Think hard."

The door chimes rang and Maggie jumped, walloping her elbow on the heavy desk chair. "Should I answer it?" she asked, rubbing her arm.

"If you don't and it's Janeen, she's likely to call the SWAT team."

"I better get it then." Maggie, with Robert close behind her, crossed the office and cut through the library to the foyer. The doorbell rang again. She peered through the peephole. "It's Officer Crosby."

Maggie opened the door, and Officer Crosby brushed her feet on the doormat, entered the room, and closed the door behind her. She was wearing a black police-issue raincoat. "It's getting nasty out there. Heard some talk earlier today about the circus opening being delayed."

"Find anything?" Officer Linton asked her.

"Nothing. I drove around a couple of blocks. Didn't see anything out of the ordinary. Couldn't find the jogger or anyone else roaming about. Came back here and checked around the shop and perimeter of the house. All clear." She wiped raindrops from her cheek. "How about you?"

"We found a mess in the office and signs of someone rifling through places in other rooms." Officer Linton looked at the staircase. "We were heading upstairs when you rang the bell."

Raindrops slid from Officer Crosby's coat and puddled on the black and white floor tiles. Maggie gestured at the coatrack. "Why don't you hang up your coat on the rack and dry off a bit?"

Officer Crosby nodded and followed Maggie's suggestion, then said, "Let's get to it."

The trio trudged up the stairs. At the top, Officer Crosby groaned. "This staircase is lovely, but I'd hate to climb it every day after my shift."

Maggie smiled. "Trust me. There are days I'm relieved my bedroom is downstairs."

Room by room, they discovered irregularities similar to what Maggie had found in her bedroom: drawers not quite closed, mattresses slightly off-center, and closet doors cracked open. But nothing was missing.

They'd gone through two bedrooms when they entered the guest suite. The blue floral curtains billowed in the breeze. Officer Crosby crossed the room to the window and pulled back the curtains. "The window's open all the way." She turned to Maggie. "Do you usually leave your upstairs windows open when you don't have guests?"

"Never," Maggie said, a lump forming in her throat. "It was closed five days ago when I came up here to store some sheets in the closet. And the cleaning people haven't been here yet this week, so they couldn't have opened it."

The dresser drawers were slightly ajar. Officer Linton opened each one. "These have been emptied."

"I keep them empty and available for guest use, like the closet."

He scribbled a few notes. "One last room, right?"

Maggie nodded. "Isn't it odd that nothing's been stolen?" She led the officers to the last bedroom, the one used for storage.

"A little," Officer Crosby said. "But theft isn't always the motive in a burglary. Could be an intimidation tactic, or they were searching for something."

A chilling thought flashed through Maggie's mind. "Could this be related to the murder outside The Busy Bean?"

"Could be." Officer Linton looked up from his notepad. "I can't say for certain, but we're watching out for you and Aunt Ina until we get this settled."

Frustration and fatigue surged through Maggie. "The man, Francesco Valli, was a stranger. I don't know anything about him. What in the world was this person looking for and why would it be in my house?"

"That is the million-dollar question," Officer Crosby said.

Officer Linton cleared his throat. "This may have nothing to do with the murder. I hate to say it, but sometimes you just never know whose feathers you might have ruffled."

"At any rate," Officer Crosby said as they descended the steps and entered the foyer, "we're going to keep an eye on the place until we find out what's going on here." She lifted her coat from the rack. "Don't hesitate to call us if anything strange happens."

"I won't." Maggie bit her lip, nervous about just how much stranger things could get.

9

Maggie poured her second cup of coffee, grabbed her cell phone from the kitchen desk in case the police called, and headed out to the porch swing in hopes the sound of the ocean would soothe her soul before more rainstorms rolled in.

She dug a paper towel from her jeans pocket and dried off a spot on the swing. Sitting down, she placed the phone beside her and clutched the cup between her hands to warm them. Inhaling, she felt the cool breeze and salty air wash over her. She prayed for peace and safety, and her thoughts drifted to the events of the past few days. What had she done to warrant someone burglarizing her home? Merely having a lunchtime conversation with a stranger had snowballed into a dangerous mess. *Who targeted Francesco? And why are they now after me?*

Her cell phone chimed with an incoming text. Maggie smiled when she saw James's name, but her face fell as she read the message. *Can't make it to lunch. Last-minute meeting.*

Maggie's hand tightened on the phone as she stared at the words. *Is James meeting with Juliet instead of keeping our lunch date?* With a sigh, she dropped the phone onto the cushion beside her.

For a few minutes, she sipped her coffee and gazed at the clouds rolling across the sky above the ocean. Watching the water from the veranda usually calmed her, but today the angry waves and gusting wind chilled her to the bone. The thought of staying home with visions of the intruder prying into her life filled her with dread. She needed to stay busy.

She grabbed her phone and called Ina, who picked up on the second ring.

"Hiya, Maggie."

"Good morning," Maggie said, hoping she sounded more chipper than she felt. "I thought I'd head to the circus grounds and see if someone can tell me if the circus poster is authentic and give me an approximate age so I can price it accordingly."

"Maggie, this poster has been rolled up for who knows how long. It's probably not worth anything."

"Oh, I forgot to tell you." Maggie shook her head at her memory lapse. "Shelley offered me a different poster yesterday. It's gorgeous. Her mom had framed it, and it's in perfect condition."

Ina cleared her throat. "I'm sure the circus management will be too busy to talk to us."

"Nope. I heard last night the opening would be delayed a day because of the rain. The morning news said something about drainage problems in the field."

"If it's too wet for performances, don't you think it's too wet for us to be sliding around in the mud with what could be a valuable circus poster?"

"Come on, Ina. You've been known to walk all over town in the rain. Where's your sense of adventure today?"

Several seconds passed before Ina spoke again. Maggie thought the wind was drowning out Ina's voice, but it was loud and clear when she broke the silence. "Oh, all right. I'll go. You don't need to be wandering around the place all by yourself. You might get accosted by a clown."

Maggie smiled and stifled a chuckle. She'd be safe enough on the circus grounds, but Ina, despite her small stature and age, was a fierce protector of her friends and family. She could always be counted on to protect her loved ones, even from theoretical danger. "Fantastic. I'm happy to have your company. I'll pick you up in half an hour." *And maybe find out why you act so peculiar about the circus.*

"By the way, I heard Robert's call about Sedgwick Manor on my police scanner last night. Thank goodness for timely rolling patrols. I was glad to hear him report 'no injuries' to the dispatcher. What exactly happened?"

Maggie accepted her friend's not-so-subtle change of subject and described the events of the previous evening, taking special care to stress she was unharmed and nothing appeared to have been stolen from the house. "Your nephew is always so kind. So is Officer Crosby. I just wish I weren't seeing them so often in a professional capacity."

"He's a good egg. I'm glad they're both keeping an eye on you."

"Me too." Maggie checked her watch. "I need to get moving so we can get to the circus."

"Yippee." Ina's voice was laced with sarcasm.

"Trust me," Maggie said, attempting to lighten Ina's mood. "It'll be interesting. Wet, but interesting."

After she had ended the call, Maggie swayed on the swing and stared at the water relentlessly crashing on the rocks. Between Ina's strange behavior, the murder, and the recent break-in, her thoughts were churning with as much force as the sea.

. . . .

Ina was waiting under the overhang outside her front door when Maggie pulled in front of the house. Her face unreadable, Ina started down the steps as soon as the Jetta came to a stop. Her gait wasn't quite as perky as usual.

"Hello, sunshine," Maggie said as Ina opened the passenger door and fumbled with her yellow raincoat while sliding into the seat.

"Oh, don't mind me. I'm just old and crotchety."

Maggie's jaw dropped. She'd never heard Ina describe herself as old. "You're the youngest seventysomething I know. By the way, I have something to show you." She dug through her purse and pulled out the trinket June discovered when they were going through the Wyeth antiques. "We found this in the game chair from Hattie's house." She held it out to Ina. "Have you ever seen anything like it?"

Ina nodded. "It's a giant's ring. I remember kids at school wearing them after the circus had been in town." She gazed through the windshield. "Evidently a giant's finger is the same size as an eight-year-old's wrist."

"I thought you might like to have it."

Ina's lips curved in an uncomfortable smile. "Thank you, but I have no need for trinkets. Perhaps you can donate it to the church childcare program. They have a dress-up station for kids."

"Good idea," Maggie said, returning the bracelet to her purse and turning the key in the ignition. "I'll do that."

Maggie chattered about Emily's phone call and speculated about possible wedding bells as Ina stared at the drenched road, making the occasional sound to indicate she was listening.

A few minutes later, Maggie coasted to a stop in front of the circus grounds and looked in her rearview mirror. "Doesn't it seem weird to locate a boisterous circus next to the silent cemetery?"

Ina shrugged. "I've never thought much about it."

Maggie shifted her attention to the circus grounds. Fascinated by the scene behind the chain-link fence, she inched the car forward and parked along a grassy strip outside the fence. A few pickup trucks, two up to their hubcaps in mud, had bulging tarps over their beds as they crossed the grounds. Men, women, and several children, some in raincoats and boots and others in rain-soaked blue jeans, sloshed through puddles while scurrying from one place to another. Four men, all dripping from head to toe, were in the process of erecting an arched gateway proclaiming, *Welcome to Circus de Vita.*

Ina stared out the passenger-side window and studied the scene through raindrops running down the glass. "Perhaps this isn't the best time to cart an old, possibly valuable poster through circus grounds."

"When would be a good time? We're lucky we have a chance at all. I'll grab the poster." Maggie stepped out of the car, thankful she'd opted to wear her old duck boots and a hooded rain jacket for the outing.

She unlocked the trunk and popped it open. The framed poster, wrapped in the towel Shelley had given her and covered by a plastic trash bag, hadn't budged during the short trip from Carriage House Antiques to the circus grounds. She had stopped by the shop briefly to pick up the poster and let June know where she was heading with it. Maggie grasped the sides of the bundle and lifted it from the trunk.

"I'll close the door for you," Ina offered.

"Thank you." Maggie raised her knee, balanced the frame on it, and repositioned her hands to bear the weight more easily. She grinned at Ina. "Nice rain hat."

Ina smiled genuinely for what seemed like the first time in ages and touched the brim of her yellow rain hat, which she had added before getting out of the car. "You know I like to be prepared," she said, shutting the trunk door.

They passed beneath the welcome sign and entered the grounds, then looked around for the manager's office. People scurried by, but no one stopped to ask if they needed help.

Ina tapped Maggie's shoulder. "See the woman moving boxes around the bed of the red truck?"

"Uh-huh. Why?"

"She's looked over here a couple of times. She's the first person who's noticed. Let's ask her for directions to the office."

Mud splattered the toes of Maggie's boots as she and Ina approached the truck. "Is that a dagger tattooed on her neck?"

Ina squinted. "I believe so."

Maggie grimaced. "Wouldn't a nice butterfly do?"

"Some people aren't into butterflies."

The bulky poster shifted in Maggie's arms. "To each her own."

The woman looked up as Maggie and Ina approached. "You lost?"

Maggie forced herself to look in the woman's unnaturally green eyes instead of at her neck. "We're trying to find the manager's office."

"Red RV, straight back," she said, pointing down the mushy path running beside a team of men attempting to erect a humongous red-and-white tent in the furious wind. Based on the men's frantic gestures and shouting, Maggie surmised it wasn't going too well.

"Thanks." Maggie turned away before she could get distracted by the dagger tattoo on the woman's neck.

"Woman of few words," Ina said as soon as they were out of earshot. "Guess the tattoo speaks volumes for her."

"Sure does."

Maggie was enthralled by the people bustling around like worker ants building a miniature city. The back of the lot was littered with RVs and semitrailers. The manager's office, the only red RV, was perched on the front edge of the community of vehicles.

Ina rapped on the door and stepped back. The drizzling rain was running off the roof of the vehicle.

The door opened a few seconds later, and a sallow face

appeared. "Yeah?" The man's lips scowled under a gray handlebar mustache tinged with yellow, which matched his curly hair.

Maggie was undaunted by his curt tone. "I'm Maggie Watson. I own an antiques shop in town. I'd like you to take a look at something for me."

"Look, lady, I'm trying to get this place up and running." Dark half-moons stretched under his eyes, and he reeked of cigar smoke.

Ina wiped raindrops from her cheek. "We'll only take a minute of your time. Is there a place we can chat out of the weather? It's rough on my old bones."

Maggie tried not to smile when she realized Ina was using her age to their advantage.

The manager's eyes softened under his bushy eyebrows. He opened the door wider. "Come in then."

"Thank you so much," Ina said. She removed her rain hat and shook the water off of it before climbing through the door and up a couple of steps into the office.

The man stood back as the women entered and stopped in front of his desk. "What's this all about?"

Maggie, trying to ignore the sound of Ina's fingers drumming on the manager's metal desk, peeled the plastic bag and towel away from the poster. "I'm looking for information about this so I can share its story with my customers." She rested the bottom of the frame on the desk and held it up so he could see the illustration better. "Can you tell me how old it is?"

He bent his head closer to the poster. Ina's drumming intensified.

"Can't say for sure. Could be from the 1950s, judging from the style and color quality." He stood up straight. "You'll need to take it out of the frame to check for a Billposters Union stamp. It could be hiding under the mat. If there's a stamp, then the poster was made after 1950 because that's when billposters became unionized, requiring every poster displayed to receive a stamp."

"How do you know this poster's authentic?" Ina pulled her drumming fingers away from the desk to tap the poster frame with her index finger.

"I've been with this circus since I was a teenager." The man smiled, his tone condescending. "I know posters—and everything else about this circus."

"I'd rather not take it out of the frame here, but I'll check later." Maggie turned her attention to Ina. "Do you remember anything like this posted by the circus when you came as a kid?"

Ina had a death grip on the side of the desk. "Nope, not my thing. Too long ago."

Maggie, sensing Ina's discomfort, asked the manager one more question. "How can I find out the names of the performers on the poster?"

"I suggest you call the Circus World Museum in Baraboo, Wisconsin. Maybe they can tell you." He gestured toward the door. "That's all the time I have for you."

Maggie quickly re-covered the framed poster with the towel and bag. Following Ina's lead, she descended the stairs, opened the door, and stepped onto the soggy ground. Turning, she said, "Thank—"

The door slammed before she could finish the phrase. She winced. "Wasn't he charming?"

"I guess the circus isn't always a cheerful place," Ina answered, stuffing the rain hat in her coat pocket. "At least it stopped raining."

"True. Charming or not, he did give us a little information and told us how to find more, so our trip wasn't wasted."

The wind whistled between the vehicles in the back end of the circus grounds, and Maggie hugged the poster closer to her body to keep it from getting caught in the wind. "I'm glad the rain stopped," she said, raising her voice above the noise. "But this wind is getting fierce."

They trudged to the car in companionable silence, both watching the process of the circus setup in progress. When they passed through the gate, Ina turned around and stared at the hustle and bustle on the other side of the fence. "I used to love the circus," she said, then resumed her trek to the car.

Maggie unlocked the car with the remote and stowed the poster in the trunk while Ina climbed into the passenger seat. Her cell phone vibrated in her purse as she closed the trunk. She pulled out her phone and peered at the caller ID. She didn't expect James to call after he canceled their lunch plans.

"Hello?" Maggie opened her car door to the welcoming quiet inside.

"Maggie? It's James. I can barely hear you." He paused. "Where are you? I've been waiting for you at The Beacon for twenty minutes. Are you all right?"

"I'm at the circus grounds with Ina. You canceled our lunch plans, remember?"

"I did what?"

"You texted me and said you had a last-minute meeting and wouldn't be able to meet for lunch today."

"Maggie, I would never cancel plans via text. It's too impersonal," James said. "If you have time, I'd still like to have lunch with you."

"I don't understand. What happened?"

"I have no idea." He sounded sincere. "I'll wait for you if you can come."

"Okay, I'll be there in ten minutes or so. I need to take Ina home on the way."

"Excellent," James said. "See you soon."

Shaking her head, Maggie ended the call. "Wonders never cease."

"Oh?" Ina cocked her head, her blue eyes twinkling. "You have a date?"

Maggie started the car and pulled out. "I'm meeting James for lunch at The Beacon. Why don't you come with us?"

Ina smiled, a sight Maggie hadn't seen much of lately. "Oh no, you know what they say about three being a crowd. I wouldn't dream of intruding on your romantic lunch date."

Maggie felt her cheeks redden as she steered the car onto the street.

It's not a date . . . is it?

He asked me to meet him at The Beacon while Juliet was lunching with their client today. But this morning he texted me and canceled our plans. Or I thought he did."

"What do you mean?"

"He says he didn't send the text." Maggie checked the rearview mirror and eyed the car that had suddenly appeared behind her and hovered too close to her bumper for Maggie's liking. Relief flooded through her when he turned right on Harbor Street as Maggie continued to go straight.

"Maggie, did you hear me?"

"Oh, I'm sorry. I was lost in thought." Maggie felt the familiar burning in her cheeks. "What did you say?"

"I said, you believe him, right?"

Maggie nodded. "He's never lied to me before, but I can't explain what happened."

"Then don't try. Go to lunch and have a good time." Ina cut her eyes toward Maggie. "I know you enjoy his company."

Maggie drove a block, lost in thought. She wanted to know why James would send the text but deny knowing anything about it. "I do enjoy his company," she finally said, crossing Cliff Road.

"Good. Let me know how you like The Beacon," Ina said. "I haven't eaten there yet."

"Will do." Maggie pulled into Ina's driveway. "I'll call the circus museum after lunch and let you know what the curator says about the poster."

Ina unbuckled her seat belt and opened her car door. "I'm more interested in hearing about your lunch with James."

10

The Beacon had recently opened in the old rope factory near the VFW, and Maggie was looking forward to trying their food after having heard good reviews. A row of large square windows stretched across the front, giving the promise of a great harbor view. The parking lot was packed, and Maggie was grateful her small car fit in the only remaining space. She and James would have plenty of company during lunch. She ran a brush through her hair and reapplied lipstick, praying she didn't look as disheveled as she felt after tromping through the circus grounds.

Maggie opened the front door and stepped into a small lobby dotted with potted plants between long, sleek, dark wooden benches. Framed black-and-white photos of harbormasters and lighthouse keepers lined the walls. The din of conversation vibrated out from the dining room.

"May I help you?" A blonde hostess smiled behind a small light on a lectern.

"I'm meeting someone. I think he's here already."

The hostess looked up as the restaurant door opened and someone approached to stand in line behind her. She nodded to the new arrival and returned her attention to Maggie. "Alderman Bennett by any chance?"

"Yes." Maggie laughed. "Are you a mind reader?"

"I wish." The young woman chuckled. "Alderman Bennett said he was expecting someone, and he described you to a tee."

Maggie was tempted to ask how James had described her but decided against it. "Where will I find him?"

"I'll take you, Mrs. Watson." As they started through the arch into the dining room, the hostess glanced behind them and spoke to the man waiting at the hostess station. "I'll be right with you, sir."

Maggie followed the hostess to a corner table in front of the last window along the front of the restaurant. James stood to greet her as she approached the table. He looked handsome in dress slacks and a blue sport shirt. She regretted not stopping by the manor to change her clothes, or at least her boots, before heading to the restaurant.

"Maggie," he said, wrapping her in a loose hug. "I'm glad you came."

"I'm glad you called." Maggie smiled and stepped out of his arms. "I'm not sure what caused the confusion."

Before he could reply, a young man with a shock of blond hair appeared at their table. "I'm Dante. I'll be your server this afternoon." He deposited a pair of menus featuring a photo of the Somerset Harbor Lighthouse on the cover. "Would you like a cup of coffee or tea while you look at our menu?"

"Just water with lemon for me." Maggie smiled. "This is a lovely restaurant."

"Thank you." Dante returned her smile. "First time here?"

Maggie nodded.

"May I suggest our brie-and-turkey sandwich with caramel-ized onions, apple slices, and applewood-smoked bacon? Or perhaps the lobster-and-scallop macaroni and cheese? They're my personal favorites."

Maggie's stomach rumbled at the thought of either of those options. "I'll keep that in mind."

Dante turned to James. "What would you like to drink, sir?"

"Water, no lemon, please."

"I'll be back with your drinks shortly."

Maggie opened the menu and browsed the options, but thoughts of James's strange text distracted her. "James, I still don't understand about the text you sent canceling our lunch plans." She lifted her cell phone from her purse and pulled up the text for him to read. "See, it came from your phone number."

"I never doubted you, Maggie." James pulled her hand closer and peered at the phone. "But I'm not sure how it happened. I assure you I did not write that text. And it's not showing up in my phone. Look." He pulled out his phone and showed her their message thread. Sure enough, she didn't see anything about canceling lunch.

Maggie looked into his eyes and was sure he was telling the truth. "I believe you."

Dante arrived with two glasses of water and a small bowl of lemon slices. "Are you ready to order?"

Maggie looked at her unopened menu, then smiled at the waiter. "You sold me on the turkey with brie and caramelized onions."

"It comes with a cup of soup. Today we have tomato bisque and seafood chowder."

"Tomato bisque, please."

Dante shifted his attention to James. "And for you, sir?"

"A business associate told me your lamb-and-eggplant shepherd's pie is incredible. Is it available today?"

"It sure is." Dante grinned. "Be sure to save room for dessert. The chef's twist on sweet potato pie is to die for."

"Poor choice of words in Somerset Harbor these days," James said as Dante scurried to the next table. "I understand there was excitement at the manor yesterday."

Maggie never ceased to be amazed at the speed with which information flew around town. "How'd you know?"

"I stopped by the police department this morning to check on the murder investigation. Chief Cole mentioned your break-in and suggested it might be related to the murder. So, what happened?"

Maggie described the previous day's events while attempting to hide the fear rearing its ugly head as she spoke. "The police department has been conscientious about sending patrol cars by the manor at regular intervals, so I know they're taking it seriously."

James's gray-blue eyes clouded. "I saw the patrol car in front of the house when Juliet and I left the antiques shop yesterday afternoon shortly after you did, but I didn't think anything about it. I knew the chief had ordered scheduled patrols on your block." He reached across the table and covered her hand with his. "Now I wish I'd stopped and checked on you before taking Juliet back to the Oceanview Hotel."

Maggie was ready for a subject change, and she was curious to know a little more about his relationship with his business partner. "How are things going with Juliet?"

"The project is moving along. If everything continues to run smoothly, we'll finish sooner than we estimated." He rapped on the polished wooden tabletop. "Knock on wood. I expect the Witmarsh Mansion to be featured in major architectural and design magazines when it's completed." James paused to take a sip of water. "Juliet is a design magician."

"Bennett Consulting is no slouch either, you know," she said with a wink, receiving a warm smile in return.

Dante approached with plates lined up one arm and a soup bowl in the other. "Here we are," he said. He placed the tomato soup in front of Maggie, followed by a plate topped with an enormous sandwich.

James inhaled with approval as the waiter set the shepherd's pie in front of him. "This is exactly what I need after a busy morning."

"Juliet's keeping you busy?" Maggie asked as Dante moved to another table and James dug into his lunch.

"She never stops, which is why we're so far ahead of schedule. I think she must work in her sleep."

"So, it's a good partnership then?" Maggie nibbled at her sandwich.

He nodded. "And a very profitable one, at that. We have a couple of other collaborations in the works in New York City and Boston."

A strange twinge pinged inside Maggie. *Is his enthusiasm for the project itself or for Juliet?*

"Have you—" Maggie's words fell off and her jaw dropped as the man she'd seen outside the printshop with Juliet approached the table.

"Maggie?" James leaned forward. "What is it?"

"A man is coming toward us. I think I saw him outside the printshop talking to Juliet yesterday. I'm pretty sure she was pointing to me as I walked to my car."

"Juliet?" He frowned.

"Excuse me." A shadow fell over the table. "Alderman Bennett, I'm Curtis Etling, a reporter with the *New York Examiner.* I'd like to talk to you and Mrs. Watson about the coffee shop murder."

Maggie groaned. "Is that what the media is calling it, the Coffee Shop Murder?"

He looked down at Maggie and ignored her question. "I know you were the last one to talk to Francesco. I need you to tell me what he said to you. What exactly did you see when you walked out of The Busy Bean?"

James stood up. "Mr. Etling, is it? I know you're trying to do your job, but we're in the middle of lunch here." He pulled his wallet from his back pocket, removed a business card, and held it out to the reporter. "Call my office and make an appointment, and then I'll be happy to talk with you."

"An appointment? You're kidding, right? I'm talking about a murder here."

"Not right now," James said with more force than Maggie

had ever heard him use. He thrust the business card close to the reporter's chest.

"But Mr. Bennett, Francesco was my—"

"Don't make me call the manager."

"I'm sorry I interrupted your hot date to discuss my friend's murder." The reporter plucked the card from James's fingers and glared at James as the manager hurried to the table. "Don't worry—you'll see me again. I don't give up that easily."

Maggie sat in stunned silence as Etling turned on his heel and nearly bumped into the manager, a slightly rotund man with dark bushy eyebrows. The reporter left the dining room without looking back.

"I'm so sorry, Alderman Bennett." The manager's voice oozed with concern. "Let me comp your meal for you."

"That's not necessary." James's face had relaxed. "We were thoroughly enjoying our lunch until the reporter interrupted us, which had nothing to do with the restaurant. The food and service have been outstanding."

"Thank you for saying so. You're very kind." The manager smiled. "I hope you'll return to The Beacon soon."

When he left the table, Maggie nibbled on her sandwich and searched for something to say. She'd lost her appetite and desire to talk. After a few bites, she pushed her plate away. "I'm sorry, I can't eat any more. The sandwich is delicious, but I've lost my appetite."

"I understand." James met her gaze. "This was hardly the lunch I'd planned when I made our reservations. I try to be cordial to everyone, including reporters, but enough is enough."

"I appreciate the invitation, regardless of how things have gone. I've been exhausted and on edge ever since Ina and I walked out of The Busy Bean and found Francesco's body on the sidewalk. Every time I turn around, something bizarre is happening." She stifled a yawn. "I'd like some peace and a full eight hours of sleep."

"I'll bet." James waved his hand to get Dante's attention.

The waiter hustled to the table. "Is everything all right?" He stared at Maggie's plate and frowned. "Oh no. You didn't like it?"

"The food was delicious," Maggie said, placing her napkin on the table. "I'll definitely be back when life is calmer."

"Excellent." Dante's face brightened. "I look forward to serving you again."

"We'll take the check, please," James said, pulling his wallet from his back pocket.

"And a box for the sandwich, please," Maggie said.

"Certainly. I'll be back in a moment."

Maggie and James sat in silence until Dante returned with the check, a medium takeout carton, and two small to-go boxes.

"Here are two pieces of sweet potato pie, on the house," he said, placing the boxes on the table. "Mr. Bristow, the manager, sincerely apologizes for the disruption to your lunch."

"No apology necessary." James stood up and set a generous tip on the table. "Please thank Mr. Bristow for the dessert."

"I will, sir. Thank you." Dante smiled and headed over to wait on two young women who were just sitting down two tables away.

Maggie put her sandwich in the empty box, then stood up and pushed her chair in. James picked up the smaller to-go boxes in one hand and placed the other hand on Maggie's back as they walked through the maze of tables.

James paused at the top of the steps outside the door. "Where's your car?"

"In the very back, next to the Dumpster." Maggie held her purse strap tighter. "The crowd has thinned out a bit since I got here."

"I'll walk you to your car." James offered Maggie his arm.

"I wasn't looking forward to walking out back alone after the terse conversation with the reporter." She took his arm and turned toward the car. "What if this Curtis Etling turns out to be a bona fide reporter looking for the truth?"

"First things first. He didn't have a press badge, which is one reason why I didn't want to talk to him in the restaurant." James glanced around the parking lot. "I want to find out if he's who he says he is."

"Should be easy enough," Maggie said. "Most newspapers have the names, and often photos, of their reporters listed on their websites."

"True enough. I'll let you know as soon as I find out any information about him."

"Likewise." Maggie pulled her keys from her purse and unlocked her car with the remote. "He said he works for the same newspaper as Francesco. If he worked with Francesco, he might be able to shed some light on why his colleague was murdered. I'd really like to know."

James gave Maggie a quick hug and opened the car door for her. "I'm rather curious myself. Call if you need me."

"I will." Maggie dropped into the driver's seat.

He handed her one of the small to-go boxes. "Enjoy your pie."

"I will." She took the box and plopped it on the passenger seat. "When my appetite returns."

11

As she buckled her seat belt, Maggie spied Ina's rain hat tucked between the passenger seat and the center console. As unpredictable as the weather had been lately, Ina was likely to need the hat sooner rather than later.

She grabbed her phone from her purse and called Ina's home number.

"Hello, Maggie. What's up?"

"I'm leaving The Beacon and I found your rain hat in the car. I thought I'd drop it by your house on the way home if it's convenient for you."

"Sure, come on by. Are you on your way now?"

"Yep. I'll see you in a couple of minutes."

Maggie ended the call and returned her phone to her purse, praying for an uneventful afternoon. She switched on the radio in time to hear the deejay giving a weather update. After returning Ina's hat, she wanted to hunker down at home to spend a few quiet hours working on repairing the antique quilt and giving Snickers some long-overdue attention. Fortunately, rain couldn't keep her from doing either.

By the time the weather forecaster had finished telling her what she'd already known—more rain would be falling over the next two days—Maggie pulled into Ina's driveway. She grabbed the rain hat and got out of the car, making sure to lock the doors before walking to the front steps.

"There you are," Ina said, opening the door as Maggie reached the bottom step. "Thanks for getting my hat back to me."

Maggie held the hat out to Ina. "You're welcome. Based on

the weather report I heard on the way over here, you're going to need it."

"Guess I won't be doing much stargazing this week with this crazy weather." Ina pushed the door open wider. "Come in for a bit."

"Storm clouds will sure put a damper on stargazing, that's for sure." Maggie stepped inside as another wave of raindrops pelted the doorstep. "But it will give you time to take the roll of film from Hattie to the camera shop to be developed."

"Oh, I can do it myself once I buy the proper chemicals. Assuming the camera shop still carries them. I used to develop all my own photos back in the day, but everything is so different now."

Maggie wasn't surprised that independent Ina wanted to do her own developing instead of entrusting her photos to a stranger. After a pause, she asked, "Ina, why don't you do photography like you used to?"

Ina stuffed her hat into the pocket of her raincoat, which was hanging on the coatrack by the door. "Want to stay for a cup of tea until the rain passes?" She waved Maggie toward the kitchen, from which a whistle called. "I put the kettle on right after you called."

"I can stay a few minutes. A cup of tea and conversation sounds nice." *Especially if it means you'll answer some of my questions.*

In the kitchen, Ina pulled a red Fiesta mug from the cabinet and set it on the counter next to its twin. She placed a tea bag into each one. "Any news on the murder?" She grabbed the kettle and filled both mugs with water.

"Nothing." Maggie carried the two cups of tea to the kitchen table and sat down. "But a reporter from Francesco's newspaper interrupted the conversation James and I were having at lunch."

"Estella Flores?" Ina asked as she took a seat across from Maggie.

Maggie shook her head. "He identified himself as Curtis Etling. He was pushy."

"What happened? Did he threaten you?"

"He was demanding enough to cause a scene. James asked him to call his office and make an appointment, but the guy wouldn't listen."

Ina sipped her tea. "What happened?" Clutching her cup between her two palms, Ina listened without comment while Maggie gave her an abridged version of the story. When Maggie stopped talking, Ina cleared her throat. "Are you sure he was really Curtis Etling? If so, did he actually work with Francesco at the *Examiner*?"

"I wondered the same thing."

"We could call the paper again and ask for him." Ina's face lit up. "I'm really curious now."

Maggie pulled out her phone. "I think I'll check the paper's website first. They'll often run reporters' photos along with their names and contact information on the staff page. I'm not ready to talk to another reporter yet, considering what happened to the last one."

Maggie launched a quick Internet search, and soon she was looking at a photo of Curtis Etling, crime reporter. "He's the real deal, all right."

"Good," Ina said, setting her cup on the table and leaning over to look at the phone screen. "At least we know that much. Oh, and he's kinda cute too."

"At least he didn't lie about his job." Choosing to ignore Ina's comment about Etling's appearance, Maggie scrolled through the paper's staff listing and found Francesco's smile staring back at her. It was the last photo on the page. *Francesco, what did you get yourself into that got you killed?* She was weary of thinking about murder and wanted to change the subject. She closed the website, her mind switching to another, more benign mystery. "Ina, why did you give up photography?"

Ina dipped a heaping spoonful of sugar out of a china bowl and dumped it into her cup. "No mystery there. The digital age took over, and it became increasingly expensive to develop film."

"So, why not go digital and keep pursuing your passion?"

Ina grimaced. "I can't capture the same heart and soul with a digital camera. Digital is fine for snapshots, but it's not what I consider fine art."

Maggie had never thought of Ina as a quitter. *Maybe developing the film will motivate her to pick up a camera again.* "I have some time right now. I'll give you a ride to the camera shop to get the chemicals you need so you won't have to worry about getting caught in the rain with an armload of supplies."

Ina sipped her tea in silence. A minute later, she lowered her cup to the table. "Maybe you're right."

Not wanting to give Ina time to change her mind, Maggie snagged both cups, took them to the sink, and grabbed her purse from the back of the chair. "The rain's stopped, so let's go now."

Ina stood. "Oh, all right. I guess there's no time like the present. I'll grab my raincoat."

She plucked her coat from the rack by the door and shrugged into it as she followed Maggie out the door and into the Jetta.

"I'm looking forward to seeing the photos after they're developed," Maggie said while they waited at a stop sign to cross Cliff Road. "This could be the beginning of a whole new photography phase for you."

"*Pfft.* You know, the more you hang around with me, the pushier you become." Ina's smile belied her grumbling. "I think I'm rubbing off on you."

"Heaven forbid there should be two Inas," Maggie said with a laugh.

Ina snickered. "Okay, I'll admit it. I'm somewhat looking forward to returning to the darkroom, as makeshift as it will be. It's been a long time since I've taken photographs, much less developed them."

"I'll bet it comes back to you like it was yesterday," Maggie said, pulling into a parking space in front of A Thousand Words Camera Shop.

"You have extraordinary faith in me, Maggie Watson." Ina grabbed her drawstring bag and opened her car door.

Maggie met her on the sidewalk. "You haven't proved me wrong yet."

Ina chuckled. "It's bound to happen at some point."

"I'm not too worried." Maggie pulled open the shop door and held it open for Ina.

Ina took several paces into the shop, stopped, and turned on the spot like a revolving lighthouse beacon, oblivious to the young woman chatting on the phone behind the front counter. "I haven't been here in decades. It's changed a little bit."

"I'll bet." Ina's awe warmed Maggie's heart.

"I started taking digital snapshots out of necessity when film processing became so expensive and supplies were more difficult to find, but I like the old way better." Ina frowned. "Some things don't need to change."

But Ina couldn't hide her growing interest in the equipment she saw lining the shelves. Browsing the aisles, she picked up packages of memory cards, cables, and camera remotes, and read about their contents with both puzzlement and grudging admiration. At one point, she picked up a book titled *New Techniques in Creating Digital Art* and leafed through its pages thoughtfully.

Maggie followed Ina around the shop, enjoying her friend's

increasing fascination with modern photography methods. *Perhaps Ina could still find the same passion for digital photography as she once had for film.*

"May I help you?" The sales clerk approached them as they stood looking into a camera display case. The clerk tucked a purple streak of hair behind her ear and smiled. "Looking to buy a new camera?"

"Oh, no. I'm studying how much cameras have changed in the last fifteen years. It's astounding." Ina paused when a buzzer announced the shop door opening. "Believe it or not, I'm here to buy chemicals for developing photos the old-fashioned way."

"You're doing what?" The girl looked at Ina as if she'd said she was going to fly to the moon on a kite.

"I found an old canister of exposed film, and I want to develop it. I know how, but I don't have the necessary chemicals."

"Oh. We have a small selection in the back, I think. Follow me." The clerk started off toward the depths of the store.

"I'm going to look at the photo albums," Maggie said as Ina followed the sales clerk. "I have years of old photos sitting around in boxes in the storage room."

"Go down this aisle the other way and turn left." The sales clerk pointed to the opposite side of the shop. "Albums and frames are along the wall."

"Thanks." Maggie followed the clerk's instructions. As she turned the corner, Maggie nearly collided with another customer. She assumed it was whoever entered the shop when the buzzer went off. "I'm so sorry," she mumbled and looked up to lock eyes with a man who looked familiar. In an instant, she recognized him as the man who was leaving the historical museum on the morning of the murder. Her heart beat wildly, her thoughts whirring at the same speed. *Could he be one of the two men who asked Ruth about the circus?*

"Eh," the man grunted and hurried down the next aisle. "Wait."

But the man kept going as if he hadn't heard her. Maggie slipped after him and tiptoed to the aisle the man had entered. She found him crouched in front of a display of memory cards, looking toward the other end of the aisle. She slipped up behind him. "Didn't I see you outside the historical society a few days ago?"

"Nah." He coughed. His voice was raspy. "'Scuse me."

"Maggie?" Ina appeared from one end of the aisle as the man disappeared out the other. "Wonders of wonders, she has everything I need. Let's check out before the rain starts again."

Maggie's heart sank. She had to let him go. "Okay." Maggie covered her irritation with a smile and peered down each aisle on the way to the register counter. She didn't see the man again. However, she hadn't heard the door buzzer, either. *Where did he go?*

Maggie paced back and forth in front of the counter while Ina paid for her supplies. She was anxious to ask if Ina had also seen the man. *Am I under so much stress that I'm seeing bad guys at every turn?*

"I'm all set." Ina tapped Maggie on the shoulder. "You can stop pacing like a caged tiger now."

"Oh good." Maggie managed a smile.

They dashed to the car through sprinkling rain and were safely inside when the drops began pelting harder. Maggie adjusted her seat belt and started the car, reluctant to leave before confirming that the man she saw was the same one from the historical society museum.

"Look." Ina stared out the window as Maggie backed out of the parking space. "Isn't that the same guy we saw outside the historical society? I'll bet it is. Looks like he's watching us."

Maggie glanced out the window as she put the car in drive.

"Yep. He's watching us all right. I saw him in the store. I even asked him about it."

"What'd he do?"

Maggie shrugged. "He grunted and walked away."

"Sure looks like him." Ina shifted in her seat and looked back at the shop. "Don't you think it's a mighty big coincidence for him to show up at the camera shop while we just happen to be there, and then to act like he wasn't at the museum?"

"Could be a coincidence, I suppose," Maggie said, attempting to be the voice of reason.

"I don't think so." Ina turned to face forward. "I'm going to add it to our crime board when we get home."

Maggie eyed the raindrops speckling the windshield. "My flyers for the fall sale should be ready by now since it's so late in the day. Do you mind if we stop by the printshop on the way to your house?"

"No problem."

Maggie was hoping this simple, everyday errand might help her take her mind off the anything-but-ordinary occurrences piling up. It was getting harder to ignore the growing sense of unease prickling in the back of her mind.

12

After a brief stop at the printshop, Maggie pulled up in front of Ina's driveway, pausing to let a jogger pass on the sidewalk before pulling in. "I'll never understand people who run in the rain and snow. Why not use a treadmill?"

"Hello!" Ina waved to the jogger, who waved back. "Where's your sense of adventure, Maggie?"

"It's not in running shoes on snowy or wet sidewalks, that's for sure," Maggie said, pulling into the driveway. "Ina, may I ask you something?"

"Okay, shoot."

"Why did you act so strange when we showed the framed poster to the manager at the circus this morning?"

Ina closed her eyes a moment. When she opened them, she turned toward Maggie. "You're not going to leave this alone, are you?" She sighed with resignation. "Come inside. I'll show you."

They walked up the driveway to the house wordlessly. Ina finally spoke after she unlocked the front door and escorted Maggie into the living room. "Have a seat. I'll be right back."

Maggie sat on the overstuffed velour sofa and studied the family photos on the coffee table. Until now, Maggie had only gotten a glimpse of the living room on the way from the front door to the kitchen, the usual gathering spot. She was glad to have a glimpse into her friend's life. Several were black-and-white photographs of her mother and father, Doris and Harold Linton. In one, they were standing in front of this very house, dressed in their Sunday best. In another, they sat on a beach with Doris holding a baby, presumably Ina, and Harold digging in the sand with a toddler, most likely Ina's older brother, Wallace.

She was studying a wedding photo of Wallace and his wife, Penny, who were Robert's parents, when Ina walked in with a poster bound to cardboard with worn and torn plastic. She held it out to Maggie and said, "Take a gander at this."

Maggie took it to the window and held it up to the natural light. She inhaled sharply. "It's the same design as the framed poster, only smaller," she said, looking from the poster to Ina. "Where did you get it?"

"Hattie's father had it in the window of his pharmacy. After the circus left town, he gave it to me because he knew I loved the circus." Ina's lip trembled. "I'll never forget that poster."

"Why?"

"Let's say that particular circus experience wasn't quite what I expected and leave it at that, shall we?"

Maggie furrowed her brow. "Did he know that?"

"No, and I never told him. He was a kind man, very humble for a politician." Ina's eyes softened. "He thought he was doing a good thing. The previous year I'd badgered him for his circus poster, but his employee took it down and threw it out the day after the show closed. I think he felt bad for disappointing me. So, I accepted this one with a smile and thanked him."

"I see." What Maggie saw was Ina hiding something. She offered the poster back. "I enjoyed looking at your family photos."

"I look at them too. It keeps a piece of my loved ones in this house."

Maggie gazed across the room into the dining area. A collage of black-and-white photographs in simple frames covered the wall over the sleek lines of a walnut midcentury modern buffet. She drifted closer and was immediately mesmerized by the photos of buildings and people of New York City: Ella Fitzgerald outside an avant-garde jazz club, Carol Channing smiling in front of the St. James Theatre, and a man and woman holding hands with a small girl between them. There were doormen and cab drivers, four nuns laughing outside St. Patrick's Cathedral, and a bride and groom in Central Park, all different races and ages. "These are gorgeous." She turned to Ina. "Did you take them?"

"I did. It was a long time ago, when I lived in New York."

"I didn't know you lived in New York. Nobody's ever mentioned it." Maggie was especially drawn to the photo of the nuns. She could almost hear them laughing. "All these images show a slice of life, the personality of New York City."

"Thank you."

"Did you like living in the big city?"

Ina gazed at a photo of a reporter, his hat and tie askew, paper and pencil in hand as he watched a man giving what looked like a heated speech in front of a *Rockefeller for President* placard. "For a while, I loved it."

"Who's the guy in the photo?"

"Governor Nelson Rockefeller on the campaign trail in 1964."

Maggie shook her head. "No, I mean the reporter. There's something special about the way you caught his intensity."

Ina bobbed her head. "That's Archie." She bit her lip. "Archie Plaines."

"Did you know him? It's interesting. The photo looks like it's of the governor, but the eye is drawn to Archie."

"Archie was a reporter for the *Examiner*. And he was pretty special."

Maggie's interest was piqued. "Define special."

Ina didn't move or speak for so long that Maggie started to worry if she'd somehow offended her friend. Finally, Ina nodded. "Why don't we sit down on the sofa? This may take awhile."

After they were settled, Maggie said, "I didn't mean to pry, but there's something different about that photo."

"During my days in New York, I was fascinated with the people and places of the city. I worked as a typist for a paper company, but photography was my passion." Ina opened a carved wooden box sitting on the coffee table. "Or it was, until I quite literally bumped into Archie Plaines while I was taking photos of a burning building. He was covering the fire for the newspaper."

She pulled a close-up photo of the reporter from the box and handed it to Maggie. "After I met Archie, I began taking photos for his news stories. His editor was so impressed with them that the paper started paying me. I quit my typist job and worked as a photojournalist for three years with Archie." Ina's blue eyes brightened. "He was the love of my life."

Maggie studied the photo of a man Ina's complete opposite: tall and dark, with brooding eyes. "Your Archie was a handsome guy."

Ina took the photo from Maggie and stared at it. "Oh, he was."

Maggie was dying to ask what happened to Archie, but something in Ina's bittersweet expression kept her silent.

"We were going to get married," Ina said, her voice wavering. "But it wasn't to be."

Maggie's heart lurched. "What happened?"

"He was such a daredevil. We went mountain climbing, snow skiing, airplane flying, cruising curving roads on his motorcycle at breakneck speeds." Ina squeezed her eyes shut. "It all ended with a freak accident because of a dumb habit of his."

"What happened?" Maggie asked quietly.

"He'd lean back in his chair and put his feet up on the desk in the newsroom. I yelled at him all the time about how dangerous it was, but he thought I was being silly." She bowed her head. "But I wasn't."

"Oh, Ina."

"One day he was leaning back in his chair, just like always. Someone came up behind him to ask him about something and startled him, and he toppled backward and struck his head on the desk."

Maggie cringed and waited for Ina to continue.

"He survived but was paralyzed from the waist down. Archie was so proud and stubborn. He didn't want to be a burden on me." Ina's eyes filled with tears. "He called off the wedding and refused to see me. He died before I could change his mind."

"So that's why you never married."

"I never met anyone who made me feel the way Archie did, so I opted to fill my life with adventures instead."

Maggie reached into her purse, pulled a tissue from a pocket-size pack, and dabbed her eyes. "Would you like one? I have plenty."

"I'm okay." Ina tilted her head and smiled. "You know, I haven't shared that story with anyone, not even Robert. I don't know what it is about you, Maggie."

"Your secret is safe with me."

The conversation waned, and Maggie didn't know what else to say, so she stood up. "I should be getting back to the manor. Thanks for giving me time to stop by the printer after we left the camera shop. It saved me a trip into town tomorrow."

"And thank you for taking me to the camera shop and badgering me to get back into the darkroom in your gentle-but-persistent Maggie way." Ina led the way to the door. "I might even spend some time developing the photos this afternoon."

"Fantastic," Maggie said as Ina opened the door. "Can't wait to see them."

Ina's lips spread into an impish grin. "I'll bet you do." She paused at Maggie's puzzled look. "Wait. I'll bet you wait."

Maggie burst out laughing, happy to see her friend's offbeat sense of humor returning. "Touché." Maggie stepped over the threshold. Water dripped from the roof of the house, but the rain had stopped. "Let me know when the photos are done."

"You'll be my first call. I promise."

"Glad to hear it." Maggie waved and started down the steps. When she reached the walkway, the front door clicked shut behind her.

"What a day," she muttered, reaching into her purse to retrieve her key chain as she approached her car.

"Mrs. Watson, wait." Curtis Etling appeared from behind the tree and loped toward her.

Maggie grabbed the pepper spray from her purse. "Stop!" She stretched out her arm and pointed the pink canister at his face. "Don't come any closer."

Etling threw his hands in the air, took a couple of steps back, and froze. "Whoa. I just want to talk to you." His hands shook. "I won't hurt you."

Maggie thrust the canister farther in front of her. "I know you won't."

"Please." Etling's voice was tinged with emotion. "Francesco was my best friend, a respected colleague. I'm trying to figure out who killed him." He lowered his hands. "I think you are too."

A battle waged in Maggie's head. Etling's body language hinted at sincerity in his words. "What do you want to know from me?"

"I know you and your friend were the last people to talk with Francesco."

"How do you know that?"

"I read the police reports. I *am* a journalist, you know. Maybe if we combine my experience as a crime reporter and your eyewitness account, then we can figure out why he was murdered and by whom." Etling glanced around them, suspicion in every motion he made. "Give me a chance. Please. Meet me someplace safe."

"I don't know how I can help you. I had one short conversation with him. That's it. And my life's been crazy ever since."

"A few minutes. That's it."

"Well, I suppose it wouldn't hurt to talk as long as it's in a public place." She lowered the canister. "We can meet at—"

"No!" Etling hurled himself toward Maggie and knocked her to the ground. Pain swept through her body as the rainwater soaked through her clothes. "What are you doing?" Maggie pushed Etling away and patted the ground beside her in search of the pepper spray. The canister was beyond her reach.

"Me?" Etling sat up and pointed toward the mailbox, where a dagger was firmly embedded in the white post. "I was saving your life."

13

The reporter scrambled to his feet. "I'll be right back. Maybe I can find whoever did this lurking around here."

Maggie sat up and collected her thoughts. She stared at the dagger jutting from the post like a macabre yard ornament. *Etling can't be all bad. He did save my life.*

She pushed herself off the wet sidewalk and stood with a stumble. The back of her head throbbed where it had smacked the concrete. Maggie reached her left hand behind her head and felt a bump forming. She held the hand out in front of her and examined it, relieved there was no blood.

"No sign of anyone," Etling said, jogging back toward her. "You okay?"

"I'm a bit scuffed, but at least I have no holes in me." She stared at the knife a moment, then looked at Etling and gave a weak smile. "Thank you. I can put up with a few scrapes and a bump on the head in lieu of being stabbed."

Maggie jumped when a door slammed. Ina scuttled down the walkway waving her cell phone in the air. "You get away from her! I'll have you arrested! The police are on their way!"

"Geez, your friend is a feisty one." Etling shook his head. "I gotta go. I'll see if I can find anyone lurking around the neighborhood." He placed his hand on Maggie's forearm. "Please, meet me at the wharf. Within the hour if you can."

Maggie hesitated a second. "I'll try," she said, but the reporter was already heading toward the thicket of trees behind Ina's house.

"Oh my goodness. Are you okay?" Ina put an arm around

Maggie. "Let's get you into the house. The cops should be here any moment."

"I'm fine. I hit the back of my head on the pavement when he knocked me down." Maggie didn't budge. "Shouldn't we stay out here to make sure the knife doesn't disappear?"

"What knife?" Ina scratched her head. "If he had a knife, why did the guy need to tackle you?"

"That knife," Maggie said, pointing to the hilt of the dagger jutting from the mailbox post. "He tackled me to keep me from being impaled."

"I'm confused." Ina looked in the direction of the mailbox and shook her head. "If he didn't throw the knife, who did?"

"I haven't a clue."

"Hmm." Ina was in detective mode. "And if he wasn't trying to hurt you, why did he run away when I came out of the house?"

"He went to look for the knife thrower, then he came back to check on me." Maggie rolled her head to relieve the ache. "I think you scared him away when you came running outside brandishing your phone."

"Chasing the knife thrower, eh? Do you know how crazy you sound?" Ina rubbed her chin. "This is all very curious, but I suppose you're right about staying out here to keep an eye on the knife."

A few moments later, a police cruiser rolled to a stop at the curb. Officers Linton and Crosby jumped out and made a mad dash to the mailbox. "Aunt Ina, we heard the call over the radio. Are you two okay?"

"I'm fine, but Maggie has a bump on her noggin."

As if on cue, an ambulance pulled up in front of the house. Maggie groaned. "I don't need an ambulance for a headache."

"Probably not, but humor us anyway," Officer Linton said.

"Let the paramedics take a quick look while Aunt Ina tells Officer Crosby what she saw during the altercation."

Too weary to argue, Maggie nodded.

Fat raindrops splashed on the driveway. "Rain's starting up again." Ina touched her nephew's sleeve. "I know someone needs to take care of the knife, but could the rest of us go in the house and stay dry?"

"I'll bag the knife," Robert said to Officer Crosby as two paramedics walked up to the group, "if you'll take my aunt and Maggie into the house."

"Maggie, do you think you can make it to the house on foot?" Officer Crosby asked.

She nodded, cringing a little in the process. "I'm feeling much better. It's just a dull throb."

Robert nodded to the medics. "Will that work for you?"

A short, bearded paramedic looked at Maggie. "Did you lose consciousness when your head hit the concrete?"

"I was stunned for a few seconds, but I didn't black out."

"Okay, but walk slowly." The paramedic took Maggie by the elbow and walked with her up the porch steps behind Ina.

The second paramedic, a tall, slender young woman holding a black bag, fell in beside Officer Crosby and they joined the parade heading back into Ina's house.

"Mrs. Watson, my name is Chuck, and my partner is Ashley," the bearded paramedic said. "Tell me what happened when you injured your head."

By the time Maggie finished describing her fall, she was sitting on Ina's living room sofa with a blood pressure cuff squeezing her arm, and Ina was in the kitchen answering questions for Officer Crosby. Robert, carrying a plastic bag containing the dagger, entered the room while Chuck watched quietly as Ashley checked Maggie's vision, physical stability, and coherence.

"I see no signs of concussion," Ashley said. She glanced at Chuck, who nodded agreement. "You'll likely have a headache for a while, though."

"Is she okay to answer a few questions?" Robert asked.

Ashley shrugged. "It's probably a good idea for her to sit for a while before trying to drive or sleep, but she's fine to answer questions. We'll just fill out our paperwork and get out of your way. We'll be in the bus if you need us."

The paramedics left through the front door, and Officer Linton sat in the leather recliner adjacent to the sofa. "Judging from how deeply the knife was embedded in the mailbox post, you're a lucky woman, Maggie. You must have as many lives as Snickers."

Maggie managed a smile. "I don't think it's a good sign that a police officer has been to my home so many times he knows my cat by name."

"How did you end up on the ground?"

"I was on my way out to the car when a man tried to strike up a conversation. With everything that's happened lately, I'm leery of strangers, so I tried to avoid him. I even got out my pepper spray to ward him off." Maggie debated how much to tell him about Etling. "He suddenly knocked me down and landed on top of me. Thinking he was going to hurt me, I was about to scream when he pointed to the knife and said he'd just saved my life. I expect he did too." Maggie stretched her neck to the side, trying to work out a kink. "I've seen him walking around downtown, though. He was outside the printshop yesterday."

"Description?"

"About six feet tall, I'd say. Sandy-colored hair. Roughly your age."

"Build?"

"Height- and weight-proportional." Maggie shrugged. "That's about all I know."

Voices filtered down the hall, and a moment later Ina and Officer Crosby walked in the room. Ina stopped in front of her nephew's chair. "How's it going in here, Robert?"

He stood up. "We're finished. Maggie, you're free to go as long as you feel like driving."

"I'm fine except for a little soreness where my head hit the driveway." She rose to her feet. "I should be going now. I certainly didn't expect to be here so long when Ina invited me in for a chat."

Ina looked doubtful. "Are you sure you don't want Robert to take you home? Your car will be safe here overnight."

The only thing Maggie wanted to do was find Etling and get some answers so she could get home to Snickers. "I'm sure." Maggie forced a smile. "I'm a big girl."

. . . .

Maggie closed the Jetta's door and gazed at the sky. The afternoon was waning, the sky dark with distant storms. She walked from the public parking lot, empty but for her car, toward the wharf, trying to decide where the reporter would most likely be waiting. Fishing boats lined both sides of the long dock, which jutted into the harbor and was lined with lobster traps. From time to time, she passed double pylons towering over the others. As she neared the end of the dock, Etling stepped away from one of them.

"Maggie, I'm glad you came." He studied her face. "Are you all right? I'm sorry I ran, but I have to be careful about who knows I'm here."

"No harm done." She returned his gaze. "Why the caution, Mr. Etling?"

"Please, call me Curtis. That knife may have been as much for me as it was for you. Francesco was onto something when he was murdered, and I intend to find out what." He held up his press badge. "I really am a reporter with the *Examiner*. Francesco was more than a colleague. He was my closest friend."

"How long did you know him?"

"We met in undergrad at the University of Southern California. After graduation, we landed in New York within a year of each other. Worked together ever since, until four days ago." Tears clouded Curtis's eyes, and he blinked them away. "Our editor sent me here to investigate Francesco's murder."

"How can I help?"

Curtis motioned to a stack of crates farther down the pier. "Let's talk by the crates. We can't be too careful."

They walked in silence until they were hidden by a wall of crates. Curtis leaned against a post and pulled a thin reporter's pad from his jeans pocket. "You and Ina Linton witnessed the murder. I need to know what you know."

"Ina and I didn't see the actual murder." Maggie gently massaged the throbbing spot on the back of her head. "We talked to Francesco shortly before he dashed out of The Busy Bean. When we left a few minutes later, he was on the sidewalk, bleeding from a knife wound. That's it. I don't know how much more help I can be."

"Don't worry about that. Focus on answering my questions."

"Okay, shoot."

"What were you and Ina Linton discussing when Francesco asked to join you?"

"We'd come from visiting the daughter of her childhood friend, Hattie Wyeth. Hattie died a few weeks ago and had left a box with Ina's name on it. We were talking about Hattie and Ina's friendship and the items in the box." Maggie closed her eyes trying to remember the rest of the conversation. "Our friend Daisy, who owns the café, mentioned the circus posters going up all over town. That's about it."

Curtis jotted down a few notes. "What was in the box?"

"Why is that important?"

"Humor me, please. I've covered murders in New York City for over twenty years."

"A box camera, an undeveloped canister of film, a circus poster, and a circus program."

Curtis looked up from his notes. "Circus again?"

Maggie smiled. "The circus seems to be a big deal around here."

"I've seen the posters plastered everywhere. I don't get the attraction, personally." He shook his head. "Who entered The Busy Bean first, you and your friend, or Francesco?"

"Francesco."

"What was he doing?"

"Wasting a window-side table with his eyes glued to his laptop screen."

The reporter chuckled. "What else did you talk about?"

"He said he was writing a book about Hollywood or something. We talked about the circus, and he said something about how many successful entertainers were circus performers first."

"Huh. I knew he was writing a book, but he'd never tell me what it was about. Said talking about it would jinx the project." Curtis tapped his pen on the pad. "What was his demeanor like?"

"Nice enough, but so nervous he dropped his coffee cup and bent down to pick it up. He became more agitated and kept looking out the window." Maggie tried to visualize the scene. "Then he received a text and bolted out the door."

"Did you see what he was looking at?"

"Two long-haired bikers." Maggie sighed and looked out over the water. "I feel like I'm in the middle of a movie or something."

"Do you remember anything else?"

Maggie concentrated on what she saw after Francesco ran

out the door. Her hand flew to her mouth. "Ina and I weren't the last people to talk to Francesco."

Curtis's eyes widened. "Who were?"

"The bikers."

"Were they outside when you left the café?"

"No, they were gone by then."

Curtis closed his pad, pushed the pen into the spiral ring at the top, and slid it into his back pocket. "You've given me a lot to go on. How can I reach you?"

"By cell phone." Maggie recited her cell phone number. "What's yours?"

"I'm sorry. I should have given you a card at the restaurant. I think my personal stake in this investigation has me off my game." He pulled a business card from his shirt pocket. "Call me if you remember anything else."

"Okay, you do the same."

Curtis held out his hand. "It's good to know you, Maggie. I'm glad we're on the same team. Keep in touch."

Maggie felt Curtis watching her as she pulled her pepper spray canister from her purse and hurried down the pier to her car.

Fatigue swept over Maggie as she drove toward Sedgwick Manor, but it morphed into relief when she turned into the circular drive and came to a stop. She stared at the house, looking for signs of anything unusual. Convinced all was calm, she trudged up the steps to the front door.

"Snickers, I'm finally home." Maggie closed the door, shrugged out of her coat and hung it on the rack, and wondered when the cat would appear. "Where are you?"

She crossed the foyer into the library and found Snickers sitting in the window, watching the birds taunt him from the bushes. "There you are." Maggie rubbed him behind his ears until he tilted his head back for her to stroke under his chin. He showed his appreciation with a rumbling, melodic purr. "I didn't expect to be gone so long."

Her head ached from its contact with the concrete, but she couldn't rest yet. She still wanted to call the museum in Wisconsin as the circus manager had suggested earlier in the day. *Was it just this morning when we stopped by the circus grounds? It seems like a lifetime ago.*

She patted Snickers's head. "That's all for now." The tabby yawned and resumed his bird-watching as Maggie went through the door to the office. She put her purse on the desk and turned on her laptop, tapping her nails on the desk while she waited for it to boot up. When it did, she typed *Circus World Museum Baraboo* into the search engine and waited. A few seconds later, she not only had the phone number for the museum's Robert L. Parkinson Library and Research Center but access to an archive of circus posters. She found a wide variety of posters, but the library didn't have any posters from Circus de Vita.

Yawning although it wasn't quite evening, Maggie dialed the library's number on her cell phone. She sighed when a voice message suggested she leave a detailed message or send an e-mail to a specified address, which she jotted on a scratch pad. Reluctant to give up, Maggie opened the photo gallery on her phone to the picture she'd taken of the poster the previous day. She attached it to an e-mail with a note asking for history and background information on the poster, including an approximate value. Under her name, she typed *Carriage House Antiques*, the address, and both her cell and shop phone numbers.

"That's it for today." Maggie turned off the computer and went into the library to read. She curled in her favorite chair, set her phone on the tobacco stand, and opened a historical novel June had recommended ages ago. Not missing an opportunity for cuddle time, Snickers jumped into her lap, snuggled in for a nap, and soon purred with contentment. Lulled by the sound of purring and her growing fatigue, Maggie gave in to sleep by the middle of the second chapter.

She jolted awake when her cell phone's ringtone pierced the silence, sending Snickers leaping from her lap. Disoriented from the abrupt awakening, Maggie groped for the phone. "Hello?"

"Maggie? It's Ina. Strange things are happening here." Ina's voice was shaky.

Maggie fought to clear her head. "What's going on?"

"After you left, I spent the rest of the afternoon in the darkroom. Shortly after I came out, the doorbell started ringing, but when I opened it, nobody was there." Ina paused.

"Then what happened?"

"Someone started banging on the back door, but the same thing happened. No one was there. Then the phone started ringing incessantly, but when I answered it, all I heard was a dial tone." Ina cleared her throat. "It's weird, I tell you. And it's driving me nuts."

Maggie sensed that this was Ina's way of asking for help without coming out and saying it. "I'll be there in a few," Maggie said. "Stay right where you are."

But when Maggie arrived a few minutes later, Ina's front door stood ajar.

"Ina?" she called, taking the stairs two at a time.

There was no answer.

14

The hairs on Maggie's neck stood on end, and she put an ear to the crack and listened. The eerie crackle of the police scanner blared from the depths of the house. Lifting the pepper spray from her purse, Maggie pushed the door open a bit wider with one foot.

"Ina? It's Maggie." She peered inside the house. The coatrack that normally stood by the door now lay on the floor in the entryway. Heart pounding, she nudged the door open even wider and found the accent table on the edge of the living room turned sideways, the phone receiver dangling off the side.

Maggie's heart beat so fast she thought it would burst, and her mind whirred with the same intensity. Every fiber of her being wanted to run through the house and make sure Ina was all right. But given the disarray, it was possible the intruder was still inside. Without crossing the threshold, she stuck her head in the door, her pepper spray poised for use, and bellowed Ina's name. No response.

Yanking her phone from her purse, Maggie dialed 911, taking slow, deep breaths to calm herself.

"This is 911, what is your emergency?"

"This is Maggie Watson, and I arrived at my friend Ina Linton's house at the corner of Cliff Road and Broad Street after receiving a disturbing phone call from her. I found the front door open. From the door, I could tell the coatrack and an accent table have been knocked over."

"Mrs. Watson, where are you now?"

"I'm right outside the front door on the steps."

"Do not go in the house. Do you have a safe place to go until police officers arrive?"

"My car is here. I can lock myself inside."

"Do that. Stay inside the car until the police officers tell you it's safe to come out."

"I will."

"Are there any suspicious vehicles in the area?"

"No."

"The police are on their way. Hang tight. Stay on the line until officers arrive."

"Thank you." Maggie took a deep breath. The police scanner crackled, and a monotone voice recited Ina's address and the phrase "possible home invasion."

Maggie shivered and bolted to her car. She climbed in, locked the door, and bowed her head to pray.

The silence was pierced by a commanding voice spilling from the phone. "Mrs. Watson, are you there?"

"Yes, I'm here." Maggie sat quietly with her head bowed and recited positive thoughts in a whisper. A sharp rap on the window popped her out of the meditation. She sat up and opened her eyes to find Officer Crosby peering through the glass.

"Officer Crosby just tapped on my car window," Maggie told the operator. "Thank you for your help." She ended the call and reached for the door handle.

"Are you okay, Mrs. Watson?" Officer Crosby stepped away as Maggie opened the door and got out of the car.

"I'm worried about Ina, but I'm fine." Maggie looked at the house as Officer Williams and Robert entered it through the front door.

"Why don't we sit in the patrol car while I get your statement?"

Maggie nodded and followed the officer to the cruiser.

When they were safely inside the car, Officer Crosby opened her notepad. "Why did you come to the house?"

"Ina called and asked me to come over. She said someone kept ringing the front doorbell and banging on the back door."

"How did she sound?"

"Frantic. Scared. I've never heard her like that."

"What did you see when you arrived?"

"Everything was quiet, but the front door was cracked open. Ina never leaves the door open."

"Did you go in the house?"

Maggie shook her head. "I peeked in the door. It looked like Ina didn't leave without a struggle," she said. "Ina would never leave without a fight."

Officer Crosby smiled for the first time. "Based on what I've seen and what Robert has said, I agree with you." She opened the car door. "Speaking of Robert, here he comes now."

Robert and Officer Williams met Maggie and Officer Crosby at the end of Ina's driveway. "That's an impressive crime board Ms. Linton has in her kitchen. And she has a police scanner too," Officer Williams said. "I think she's been watching a lot of cop shows."

Maggie ignored the comment. "Ina and I created the board after the murder outside The Busy Bean." She cut her eyes to Officer Crosby. "We felt we had a personal stake in things."

"Very impressive." Officer Crosby grinned. "Have you ever thought about joining the police force? You seem to have a knack for solving mysteries."

Maggie shook her head. "I think I have enough excitement in my life without looking for it." She turned to Robert. "Any idea where Ina could be?"

He shook his head. "I hoped you might have an idea. I know you've spent a lot of time with her over the last few days."

"We talked about the murder. Went to the circus grounds to do some research on an old circus poster I purchased. I gave her a ride to the camera shop because it was raining." Maggie hesitated.

"Why doesn't Ina drive? She's one of the most independent women I know. Her aversion to driving seems at odds with her nature."

"I asked my father about it one time." Robert shrugged. "He said Aunt Ina never explained it. But you're right. It doesn't fit her personality at all."

"Back to the investigation at hand, I have a question," Officer Williams said, brushing Robert aside. "Do you know anything about the photos hanging on a line in the upstairs bathroom?"

"I haven't seen them, but I know she found the film in a box left for her by her friend Hattie Wyeth," Maggie explained. "Hattie passed away a few weeks ago, and the family is cleaning out the house."

"There appear to be three or four photos missing. Any idea who'd want them or why?"

"Haven't a clue." Maggie tucked a piece of hair behind her ear. "Ina was evasive when I asked about the items in the box."

"One more thing," Officer Williams said. "Did you walk around to the back of the house after Ms. Linton didn't answer the door?"

"No, didn't even think about it." Maggie shrugged. "Why?"

"Because we found a rappelling rope hanging from her window," he said.

"A rappelling rope? Ina's tried a lot of interesting hobbies, but I've never heard her mention rappelling."

Officer Crosby motioned Officer Williams over to the police cruiser.

They chatted a minute, then Officer Williams came back and told Maggie she could go. "Do you want us to escort you home?"

"I appreciate the offer, but I'll be fine. I'm going to call the church before I go. I'm sure Pastor David will want to start a prayer chain or something, so I might head over to Old Faith instead of home."

Officer Williams nodded. "We'll be here for a while, but don't leave without telling us."

Maggie returned to her car and called Liz Young, her good friend and the pastor's wife, and described the day's events. "I thought you and Pastor David might want to plan something to help Ina's friends and loved ones through this time while the police are investigating her disappearance."

"Oh Maggie, how terrible. I'll talk to David about activating the phone tree and recruiting the historical society to organize a vigil at the church immediately."

"I like that idea," Maggie said. "I'll let Robert Linton know and then head to the church from here. It's sweet of you to do this for Ina's friends and family."

Maggie returned to the group of police officers gathered by their cruisers. She told them about the vigil the church was organizing and let them know she'd be there if they needed to find her. Maggie walked to her car with a heavy heart and dragging feet. The three-block drive to the church seemed like thirty miles.

· · · · · · · · · · · · · · · · ·

"Oh Maggie, you must be exhausted." Liz hurried across the parish hall and welcomed her with a hug. "I've already contacted everyone at the historical society. They'll all be here soon. In the meantime, I've put on a pot of coffee and raided the pantry for snacks to nibble while we plan the vigil."

"Good idea," Maggie said, although food was the last thing on her mind at the moment.

As if on cue, Ruth, June, Daisy, and Fran filed into the hall and made a beeline for Maggie. Leading the pack, June reached Maggie first and wrapped her in a bear hug. "You've been through the wringer this week, but we're all here for you. Don't forget it."

"I'm okay. Ina's my top concern now." Maggie waved her hand at the counter where Liz was arranging coffee cups, plates, and a tray of cookies. "Thanks for coming. Let's get to work."

Armed with cups of coffee and cookies, the ladies gathered around a table, where Liz had placed a pad and pencil in front of each chair. "We'll divide the labor and hopefully have the vigil running by eight o'clock tonight. I've already contacted Joseph Miles, our youth minister of music. He's rounding up high school and college musicians to provide low-key music to keep everyone motivated." Liz, whose pad already had several lines of notes on it, picked up her pencil. "We'll need refreshments to keep people going."

"That's my territory," Daisy said. "I'll round up drinks and snacks, chips and stuff. I'll also call Clair Gregory. Maybe she'll donate bakery items."

"We need to get the word out," Fran said. "I'll get that started with the church phone tree. We'll also need a couple of people to man the phone lines in case people call for information or to offer tips."

Ruth waved her pencil. "I'll help with that."

"I will too," Maggie said, Ina's friendship outranking her fatigue. "June, would you create a flyer since you're so good at them?"

"Sure." June scribbled on her pad. "I'll look through my photos. There's bound to be a good one of Ina. I'll include information about the vigil and a phone number for people to call for information or report tips on Ina's whereabouts. I'll distribute them too. And I'll call the local radio and television stations."

Fran raised her hand. "I'll help hand out flyers."

"I think we have everything covered." Liz checked her watch. "It's about six o'clock. If we get moving now, we can meet that eight o'clock goal. We'll keep it fairly simple and unstructured with Joseph keeping music going and David leading the candle lighting at, say, ten o'clock?"

The door to the parish hall opened and Rupert Tinsdale, the church janitor, entered with an armload of telephone equipment. "Excuse me, ladies. I'm here to set up a phone bank. Where do you want it?"

"Ruth and Maggie, come with me and we'll work out the phone tree and bank." Liz stood. "I'll see the rest of you back here as soon as your tasks are completed."

. . . .

Maggie stood in the breezeway between the chapel and parish hall clutching a cup of coffee and watching the crowd gather in the grassy area in front of the church. Somerset Harbor had come out in full force to support Ina Linton, the short and sassy fireball with the biggest heart in town. *Oh, Ina, where are you? Keep the faith, my friend. We will find you.* Maggie scoured the familiar faces of friends and customers for strangers. She'd once read that murderers and kidnappers often attend vigils held in honor of their victims. *Could Ina's kidnapper be hiding in plain sight?*

A news crew from the Portland TV station had arrived thirty minutes earlier and now scurried around filming the event and interviewing Ina's friends and family as well as concerned citizens. June moved among the crowd distributing flyers that contained Ina's photo and a hotline number to call in case she was spotted. Maggie had worked the phone tree until the news crew had arrived. Now she was taking a break and dodging the camera.

"Liz thought I might find you here shirking the limelight," James said, walking up and hugging Maggie briefly. "Is there anything I can do?"

She shook her head. "I'm hanging in there. I'm glad you're here, though."

"I'm here too." Juliet appeared from behind James. She locked arms with him and dropped her head on his shoulder, staking her claim.

Maggie was spared from commenting when her phone rang from her pants pocket. But before she could answer it, Daisy sauntered up and put an arm around her. Juliet led James toward the news crew.

"For colleagues, those two sure are spending an awful lot of time together."

Maggie ignored the pang she felt watching them walk away. "They're dedicated to their project." She leaned into Daisy to fight her growing fatigue. "And obviously they like each other."

"James would be a fool to fall for her." Daisy grimaced. "That woman is a barracuda under the Balenciaga."

. . . .

The phone on the table in front of Maggie blurred. She closed her eyes and pressed her fingers to them to clear her vision.

"Maggie?" Liz placed a hand on her shoulder. "It's late. You've been at this a long time after a rough day. Why don't you go home and get some rest? We've got plenty of people to work shifts until tomorrow morning."

"Excellent idea." Officer Crosby, who'd been standing nearby chatting with James and Juliet, strode to the table. "Do you have someone who can stay with you until we locate Ina and determine who's behind her disappearance?"

"No." Maggie shrugged, an attempt to seem more confident than she felt. "All my friends are here, and Emily is in Boston. I'll be okay alone at the manor."

James cleared his throat. "I'll take Maggie home and make sure she's safe."

"But James, we have work to do," Juliet whined, running

her fingers up and down his arm. "We've already wasted too much time here."

"I'm sorry you feel this is a waste of time," James said as he disentangled himself from Juliet's grip, an edge to his voice. "Maggie's well-being is more important than work at the moment. I'll drop you by the Oceanview Hotel on the way to Sedgwick Manor."

"Don't bother." Juliet followed a hunky news anchor with her eyes, cast a dirty look at James, and scurried after the apparent new object of her desire.

"It's okay if you want to go after her," Maggie said quietly.

"The only thing I want to do is get you back to Sedgwick Manor safe and sound."

Maggie sighed. "Thank you, James. I am tired, and I want to make sure Snickers is okay."

June placed a stack of paper on the table beside Maggie's phone and yawned. "I need to crash too. Can I catch a ride with you? I left my car at the shop and rode with Fran to distribute flyers."

"Sure," Maggie and James answered in unison.

Officer Crosby walked with them out of the parish hall and around the crowd of people on the lawn. "I'm going to follow you home and make sure everything is secure there."

"My car is over here." James pointed to the far end of the parking lot.

Maggie turned back to the crowd of people who had gathered to pray for Ina. Standing on the edge, bathed in moonlight, was the long-haired woman Maggie had seen at the police station and entering The Busy Bean during the newscast about Francesco. *Could she be the one who had been waiting for me in the shadows outside the manor?*

. . . .

"Snickers, come here, boy." Maggie paused under the chandelier in the entryway, expecting the cat to scurry through the library door. She went through the library to the office, but the cat wasn't there. Fighting panic, Maggie wished she hadn't declined Officer Crosby's invitation to check inside the house. "Where are you?"

"I'll look upstairs." James disappeared up the staircase.

"I'll try the laundry room." June headed off in another direction.

Maggie's heart rate jumped as she hurried into the kitchen. She saw no signs of her cat. "Snickers? Where are you?" she called, her eyes welling with tears as she entered the breakfast room. She stood in the center of the room, closed her eyes, and sent up a prayer.

She heard a meow.

Maggie's eyes flew open. There was Snickers, stretching in the doorway to the living room. He nonchalantly sauntered over to her. She scooped him up and buried her face in his fur. "Ugh, you silly cat. I'm not letting you out of my sight the rest of the night."

"No sign of the cat up—" James stopped midsentence as he entered the living room with June on his heels. "Excellent, you found him."

"Everything is fine." Maggie rubbed the top of Snickers's head. "I'll go put fresh sheets in a guest room upstairs."

"No need. I'm going to sleep right here on the living room sofa. I want to be closer to you in case something happens."

June yawned and rubbed her eyes. "I'd better get going. I hope I can stay awake long enough to drive home."

"I'd feel better if you stayed here tonight," Maggie said. "You can stay in the guest room and open the shop after a good night's sleep."

With a tired smile, June said, "I'll take you up on that." She pulled her cell phone from her jacket pocket. "I'll call Kurt and let him know. And you don't need to change the sheets upstairs. I know you—the sheets are fine. Go to sleep. Good night." She ducked out of the room.

Maggie carried Snickers to the master suite doorway, then hesitated and turned around to face James.

"Go to bed, Maggie," he said. "I won't let anyone get near you or Snickers. I promise."

She nodded. "Thank you for being here. I'll sleep better now."

15

Maggie woke before dawn to the aroma of coffee brewing and the soothing sound of Snickers purring on the pillow next to her. She rolled over and scratched the tabby behind the ears. Then she remembered Ina's disappearance.

Wanting to return to the vigil as soon as possible, Maggie took the quickest shower of her life and threw on a pair of jeans and the *St. Joseph's College Mom* sweatshirt Emily had given her for Christmas as a freshman. When she padded into the kitchen, the sky was lighter, and James was beating eggs while bacon sizzled on the stove. He'd already set three places on the small table.

"Oh, the bacon and coffee smell amazing." Maggie grabbed a pottery mug from the cabinet and filled it with coffee. "I can't believe I slept so long."

"I can," James said, sliding a fork under a slice of bacon and flipping it. "You had a wild day yesterday."

"Why didn't you wake me earlier so I could help with breakfast and we could get back to the vigil?"

"Because you needed rest." He turned another piece of bacon. "I'll have the eggs and bacon done in a few minutes."

"Have you heard anything?"

"Pastor David texted an hour ago and said people are still keeping vigil, but he hasn't gotten any news from the police." James transferred the bacon to two plates with a spatula and poured an egg mixture into the pan. "Evidently, Robert Linton has been there all night and didn't know anything new, either."

"My father always says, 'No news is good news.'" Maggie sipped her coffee. "I have to believe he's right."

James looked up, still stirring the eggs. "We must keep the faith, Maggie. We'll find Ina."

They fell into companionable silence, each of them lost in private thought. While saddened and frightened by Ina's disappearance, Maggie was comforted by James's confident and caring presence. She'd drifted off to sleep with his promise, *I won't let anyone get near you or Snickers*, echoing in her mind.

"Breakfast is served," James said, sliding eggs onto the plates and carrying them to the table.

"I can't believe I'm hungry. I didn't want to eat a thing last night." Maggie sat down and picked up a fork. "The sleep helped my nerves, I think. Any sign of June yet?"

"Not yet." James grabbed a piece of bacon. "I'll leave a plate for her if she doesn't surface before we leave. After we finish eating, we can head to the church and see what's happening."

"Sounds good." Maggie took a sip of coffee and peered at James over the rim of her mug. "What about Juliet?"

"I texted her earlier and told her I wouldn't be at the Witmarsh Mansion today." His face was intense. "I said I want to be available in case I'm needed during the search for Ina."

"And she was okay with that?"

James smiled. "She prefers being in control, but she'll rise to the occasion."

"I figured her for a take-charge type," Maggie said.

"You figured right, but she's an excellent space planner, so people make allowances for her quirks."

Always interested in information she could apply to her own business, Maggie listened intently while James described the antique wonders he'd found at the Witmarsh Mansion. When he stopped talking, both plates were empty, and James carried them to the sink. "Go take care of what you need to do before we leave, and I'll load the dishwasher."

"Okay, thanks." Maggie left James with the dishes and returned to her bedroom to put on a bit of makeup and change her clothes. She liked how comfortable she was with James seeing her in old clothes and sans makeup.

Fifteen minutes later, she returned to the kitchen in a clean pair of jeans and a cable-knit sweater. "I'm ready to go," Maggie said, slipping the strap of her purse onto her shoulder. "Or maybe not. This is really heavy. I should take a few things out if I'll be carting it around during the vigil."

She set the purse on the kitchen desk and removed her business card case, a makeup compact, a container of mints, and sunglasses rendered unnecessary by the rain, and stuck them in the desk drawer. She left her wallet, car keys, a package of tissues, and her trusty pink pepper spray canister.

She dug her hand into the purse one more time in search of other items to remove. "What in the world?" Maggie pulled a bright-green thumb drive from the bottom of her purse. She turned it over in the palm of her hand and shivered. *Francesco Valli* was scrawled across the plastic in black permanent marker.

James peered over her shoulder. "What are you doing with Francesco Valli's thumb drive?"

"Good question. I only spoke to him a few minutes." She ran a finger over Francesco's name. "I haven't the slightest idea how this ended up in my purse."

"Think back on those few minutes, Maggie. Maybe you'll remember something."

Maggie closed her eyes and visualized walking to the table in The Busy Bean with Ina. "Francesco was working on a laptop when we sat down."

"Alone?" James prompted.

"Yes, alone."

"Was there a thumb drive sticking out of the computer?"

"I didn't see one, but I wasn't looking for it." Maggie let her mind roll like a film in a movie theater. "A few minutes later, he packed up his laptop and asked to join our table."

"Then what?"

"He asked Ina if she'd ever met anyone at the Circus de Vita when she was younger."

"Her reply?"

"I think she said 'Not really' or something nebulous like that."

"What happened next?"

"He looked out the window, saw the motorcycle guys, and became agitated. He knocked his coffee cup to the floor and bent down to pick it up."

"Did you watch him?"

"No, but he bumped into my purse, and it jiggled a little bit as he picked up his cup." Maggie's eyes flew open. "He must have slipped the thumb drive into my purse."

"If you're right," James said, reaching for the small green rectangle, "I think we need to look at what's on the drive before we return to the church."

"You read my mind." Maggie headed out of the kitchen. "My laptop is in the office."

"Let's go."

Excitement coursed through Maggie as she led James to Aunt Evelyn's old office. "What do you think is on the drive?"

"I couldn't even venture a guess since I never met the guy."

Entering the office, Maggie went straight to the desk and fired up the laptop. James handed her the drive. "Okay, here goes," she said, inserting the drive into the computer.

Maggie opened the first file in the list. "This looks like notes for his book," she said, scrolling through the document.

"Check this out." James pointed to a bullet point on the second page. "For some reason, he was looking for performers of a specific show in Somerset Harbor during 1955."

"That would explain the question he asked Ina." Maggie inhaled sharply. "The program Hattie left for Ina was from that year. Do you think that could be a coincidence?"

"My gut says no, but we need more to go on." James leaned closer to the computer screen. "Look at this," he said, pointing to a line near the end of the page. "He planned to check out the old circus site on the north side of the cemetery. He seemed to think he'd find clues to the past there."

"Here? In quiet little Somerset Harbor?" But the idea sent a current of excitement through her. "I wonder what he hoped to find."

James stood up and looked down at Maggie. "I suppose now you want to take a detour by the railroad tracks before going to the church."

Maggie removed the drive from the USB slot and shut down the computer. "How did you know?"

James pulled his car keys from his pants pocket. "Because you're incorrigible when it comes to sniffing out a mystery."

. . . .

The morning sky was darkening with distant storms as James pulled his car off the road near the old cemetery in search of Francesco's clues to whatever mystery he'd been chasing. Just south of the well-maintained, rolling hills of the historic cemetery and far beyond the athletic fields, the old circus grounds sat along the railroad on the far side of a sizable, unkempt embankment.

"I wonder who owns this property," Maggie said, wading through the knee-deep grass. "They need to hire a lawn service."

"The railroad owns twenty-five feet from the center line of the track," James explained. "Not sure about the rest, but we can look it up on the property appraiser's website."

They scrambled to the top of the embankment and looked

down the slope to the railroad tracks. Maggie studied the scenery as far as she could see in each direction. The cemetery dominated the view to the right, and thick woods were off in the distance to the left. "Not much to see, is there?"

James raised his arm and pointed right. "Not much except the two eyesores close to the back edge of the cemetery."

"It's a shame they weren't preserved." Maggie studied the two matching brick buildings, which were in shambles.

"I don't know why they didn't restore them when the depot moved farther out of town years ago." As town alderman, James prided himself on knowing historical details. "Maybe it was because they weren't the original buildings."

"What happened to the original depot?"

"It burned back in the 1940s. For some reason, it was replaced with these two."

"I wish we knew what Francesco was looking for." An image of the reporter's body sprawled on the sidewalk outside The Busy Bean flashed through Maggie's mind. "He certainly paid dearly for it."

"He sure did." James frowned. "This is a large, secluded area. I suppose there could be something buried out here."

"Like a body?" Maggie's mind was still on murder.

"Maybe. Or evidence of some sort."

Maggie weighed their options. "Well, there are only two buildings to search and who knows how many square feet of earth to dig up, so I vote to start with the buildings."

"Sounds like a plan to me," James said, starting down the slope at an angle toward the old depot.

As they trudged closer, the grass gave way to a narrow rocky path strewn with a trail of cigarette butts.

"Was your Francesco a smoker, by any chance?" James kicked a cigarette butt. "Maybe he was hanging out here."

"I have no idea. He didn't smell like cigarette smoke." Maggie looked James in the eye. "And he wasn't *my* Francesco. I only knew him about five minutes."

"He sure has impacted your life for someone who was only in it for a few minutes."

"No kidding," Maggie said. She halted and put a finger to her lips as they approached the building. "I think I hear voices."

As they crept closer to the first building, Ina's voice filtered through the football-size hole in the window. "You boys don't have the slightest idea of the trouble you're getting yourselves into. Why, if your mothers—"

Maggie smiled in spite of her fear for Ina. She wasn't surprised her spitfire friend didn't shy away from setting a hoodlum straight. She straightened up and peered in the window. A chill ran down her spine. Ina's hands and feet were bound, and she was strapped in a chair. A twisted scarf encircled her neck and rested on the collar of her shirt.

"Shut your trap. You hear me? I'm getting tired of you running your mouth." A burly man with spiked hair and an unrecognizable accent waved a gun in front of Ina. "I'll shoot you, old woman."

"Ha!" Ina glared at the hoodlum. "If you do, my Archie will haunt you until the day you die."

"I ain't afraid of no Archie," he growled.

Ina lifted her chin. "Well, you should be."

"Geez, Spike, just put the gag back on her so we can have some peace and quiet," a deep voice said. "I never heard a woman talk so much."

James motioned for Maggie to squat down out of sight. She shook her head and peered through the window again. A second man, who must have been the one who mentioned gagging Ina, sat along the wall scraping under his nails with the blade of a knife, his wild hair falling to his elbows. The hair. Where had she seen that hair?

Talking to Francesco outside The Busy Bean, that's where. Right after he freaked out and spilled his coffee.

Her eyes focused on Ina, Maggie reached into her purse and grasped her phone. As she raised it to her right ear to call 911, the cold steel of a knife blade pressed against her neck. Hot breath coated her ear.

"Drop the phone or I'll cut your throat."

16

Maggie couldn't place the voice or determine if it was male or female, but she obeyed its bone-chilling command. She released her phone, and it dropped to the grass by her feet. In the next moment, her right arm was twisted behind her back by her nameless, faceless assailant. Maggie groaned as her arm was wrenched higher against her spine and her body was turned and shoved through the door of the building.

The two henchmen stood up and stepped toward her, but they stopped when Maggie was thrust to the dusty floor. "Her boyfriend is on the ground outside," the voice snarled. "Take care of him."

The man named Spike stepped around Maggie. "What do ya want us to do with 'em?"

"You and Mick bring him in here and toss him in the corner," the leader ordered. "He won't give me any trouble."

The men nodded and stomped outside, not bothering to pull the door shut behind them.

Maggie rubbed her smarting shoulder and grimaced. She looked around the place to get her bearings and shuddered. The room was damp, dirty, and chilled from the morning air. Red walls showed behind peeling white paint. Empty fast food bags and cups littered the floor in one corner of the room. The smell of mold clung to the air with a vengeance.

Several feet away, Ina leaned her head to one side and moaned. Maggie feared her friend was weak from lack of sleep and food. If she passed out, she might tip the chair over and get hurt. "Ina, are you okay?" Maggie rose to her knees and started crawling to her.

"What do you think you're doing?" Their captor nodded toward the door. "Do you want the same treatment your boyfriend got?"

"What did you—"

Before she could finish asking what they'd done to James, Maggie was spun around and shoved to the floor. "Quiet!" her mystery captor hissed.

Maggie rested a moment to catch her breath. She struggled to a sitting position and looked at her friend. Ina's body drooped with fatigue, but Maggie was relieved to see her usual spark blazing in her eyes.

She couldn't say the same for James, who appeared lifeless as the henchmen half-dragged, half-carried him through the door and thrust him into the corner of the room behind Ina. He lay crumpled in a heap near the wall. He'd landed on his side, his legs bent and his head resting on one outstretched arm. Even out cold he was handsome. His gray slacks were streaked with dust and grime. She grimaced from a pang of guilt. James had only been trying to protect his friends, and now he was hurt. He didn't deserve this. She had dragged him into it. Powerless to help Ina and James, frustration coursed through Maggie. *Who are these strangers and what do they want with us?*

Maggie twisted and looked her captor in the eyes. "What have you done to James? He looks drugged." In an instant, she recognized Ina's kidnapper. He was the man she and Ina had seen bounding down the stairs of the historical museum before they'd met Francesco at The Busy Bean.

"Relax, nosy. Your boyfriend will wake up. Eventually. Just a little trick of the trade using a pressure point, not that you're in any position to be asking questions." He turned to the henchmen. "Why don't you make yourselves scarce for a while?" The way he said it, it wasn't a suggestion.

"Whatever you say, Alex," Spike said. "I could use a smoke break."

"Take your time," Alex replied, his smile unsettling. "I plan on enjoying every second of exacting revenge for the curse this woman brought on our family."

The two men trudged out the door, leaving it cracked an inch or two. Maggie clasped her purse against her side and considered how to extract her pepper spray and use it before the henchmen returned. But Alex was focusing on her at the moment, so the pink canister remained hidden.

"Alex, is it?" Maggie prayed her voice wasn't shaking as much as her insides were quaking. "Weren't you at the historical museum a few days ago?"

"What's it to you?" The voice was icy.

"Not a thing. Just thought I saw you."

"Are you sure it was me you saw?" Alex didn't wait for an answer, but peeled off the mustache and tugged off a brown curly wig, revealing sleek, close-cropped, jet-black hair. "After all, appearances can be deceiving."

Maggie's eyes widened when she realized what she was seeing. *Alex is a woman!*

Alex grabbed her bulky sweater by the neckline with one hand and the front of her pants with the other and yanked. Both pieces of clothing broke away from her body to reveal a tight-fitting black tunic and matching leggings. A tool belt stocked with spikes, darts, knives, and hatchets encircled her waist.

Maggie scrambled backward, her heart racing and eyes focusing on the belt. How had she gotten in the middle of what felt like a big-screen thriller?

Alex tossed the disguise aside. In a single fluid motion, she pulled a knife from her belt and hurled it across the room, where it landed dead center in a penny-size patch of mold on the wall.

Ina gasped while Maggie's jaw dropped. Alex's talents as a quick-change artist and a knife thrower had rendered Maggie speechless, and she couldn't tear her gaze away from the woman. Would they get out of here alive?

Alex's diabolical laugh echoed through the empty building. "Surprised, are you?"

Maggie stared at the knife now firmly embedded the wall.

"Each one of you," Alex added, "is a much larger target than a speck of mold. Don't test my patience."

Did this lunatic read my mind? Maggie had to ask the question burning inside her. "Why did you kidnap Ina?"

"Because someone must be held accountable."

"What for?" Ina's voice was strong, determined. "Who are you?"

"So many questions, so little time." Alex whirled to face Ina, her green eyes blazing. "You see, I've waited three lifetimes—my grandfather's, my father's, and mine—for this moment. It's time to make you pay."

"Pay for what?"

"The sins of the past."

Ina didn't take her eyes off Alex. "Whose sins?"

"What's that? A bit of memory loss? Old age creeping in?" Alex cackled. "Funny—my family doesn't seem to have that problem. Three generations of us remember."

Ina cleared her throat. "Why don't you tell us who you are and what you want?"

The woman glided toward Ina, stopped an inch from her chair, and lowered her face so it was level with Ina's. "I am Alex Lupei, granddaughter of the once-renowned trapeze artist Emil Lupei, star of the Circus de Vita!" She thrust her right hand under Ina's chin and circled her neck with her thumb and forefinger. "That's who."

Confusion and pain made Maggie's head spin. "What does this have to do with any of us?"

Alex's eyes flashed and her nostrils flared. She stood up straight and paced between Ina and Maggie like a caged tiger. "My grandfather was destined for greatness and glory until Marco Cavallo wiped him off the map all those years ago. Right here in Somerset Harbor."

Alex whirled around and sent an ax zooming within an inch of Ina's face. "And she helped."

Maggie jumped, but Ina didn't flinch, not even as the ax plunged with a thud into the wall behind her. She sat still and didn't say a word, but her chest rose and fell rapidly.

Maggie's first impulse was to dash to Ina's side, but Alex's hand hovered over the weapon belt, so she remained where she was and tried to stay as still as possible.

In the corner, James moaned and opened his eyes, then turned his head toward Maggie. They held the question Maggie had been asking herself from the second the knife was pressed against her throat: *How will we get out of here alive?* Even if James wasn't permanently wounded by whatever Alex did to him, could the two of them find a way to overtake an agitated professional knife thrower without getting them all killed? Even healthy, they wouldn't be a match for someone with Alex's skill.

Maggie shook her head once and pleaded to him with her eyes. *Don't move. Don't attract her attention.*

His nod was slight, and his eyelids drifted shut. Maggie exhaled slowly. James understood.

Ina's eyes fixed on Alex. "I don't know the name Marco Cavallo. I didn't know your grandfather, either, but I think I've heard of him." She closed her eyes a moment, then opened them to look Alex in the eye. "I'm so sorry."

Alex cackled. "Oh, you only think you're sorry now. You foolish old woman. You've only begun to regret interfering in other people's business."

Memories from the last few days flashed through Maggie's mind: Ina's strange reaction to the box Hattie left her, her reluctance to visit the circus grounds, her aversion to the circus posters. *It's not my imagination. Something did happen to Ina at the circus. But what?*

James stirred and sat up, color returning to his face. He blinked, scooted back to lean against the wall, and looked up at the window. Maggie followed his gaze, catching a glimpse of movement, a woman's face. She struggled to keep her expression blank, her mouth closed. She looked down. *I know that face.* The countenance in the casement was the same one she had seen in the moonlight outside the manor after she and Ina called the *New York Examiner*. *Whoever you are, please be here to save us.* When she dared another peek at the window, the face was gone. So was Maggie's hope.

Alex spun, plucked a dagger from her belt, and fired it toward James. The knife missed his cheek by a centimeter and landed in the joint where the walls met behind him. He leaned back and braced himself with the opposite arm, his face pale again. He met Maggie's gaze, and she was sure they shared the same thought: *If Alex wanted him dead, he would not be breathing.*

"Sudden movements startle me," she snarled. "You really don't want to startle me." Alex smirked at Maggie. "See, I told you he'd wake up. But I can snuff him out again just like that," she said, snapping her fingers.

Maggie couldn't take her eyes off the dagger hilt protruding from the wall behind James. Alex was taunting them now, but she'd really tried to kill her outside Ina's house. Curtis had saved her. Maggie was sure of it now. She'd been right to meet with him.

She tore her gaze from the knife when Alex danced toward Ina, her fingers brushing over the tops of the weapons encircling her waist. "Do you have any idea what you did to my family?

The blight you put on our legacy? By the time it got to me, my birthright was threadbare."

Maggie shifted position and visualized Francesco's notes. The name Alexandra, no last name, had been listed with a question mark by it. *Was she a member of the circus family Francesco had been seeking to interview for his book? It would account for her unusual talent.*

Alex's hand hovered between a spike and a knife. "You and Marco nearly killed my grandfather. You destroyed his career, his marriage, his zest for life." In a flash, her hand plucked a knife from the belt and hurled it toward Ina. "The destruction trickled down to my father, a drunkard and coward. As my grandfather always says, 'The apple doesn't fall far from the tree.'"

Ina's eyes widened and her mouth gaped, but she remained otherwise unflinching and apparently oblivious to the knife that had just whizzed by her head.

"Your grandfather says?" Ina stammered. "You mean he's alive?"

17

"Why so surprised?" Alex laughed sharply. "Thought you killed him, did you? Maybe he would have been better off if you had. He would have died a legend." Alex pulled a knife from her belt and pressed the blade against Ina's neck. "Instead, his career was ruined, our family name blackened. But he's alive and living, if you can call it that, in the Big Apple. Unlike your friend Francesco."

"My friend?"

With Alex zeroing in on Ina, Maggie stole a glance at the window. The woman outside covered her mouth with her hand, her eyes wide with shock. She remained frozen in place for a moment, then disappeared. *Please be calling the police*, Maggie begged in silence.

"Yeah, your friend Francesco Valli. Remember him?" She jerked her head in Maggie's direction. "The man you and nosy over there had coffee with before he impaled himself on my dagger." Alex pulled the knife from Ina's throat and ran her finger along its blade. "Wanna see how sharp this knife is?" Without waiting for an answer, she slipped the blade inside Ina's collar and sliced along the shoulder seam as though it were soft butter.

Ina's nose twitched, but her eyes stared straight ahead.

Anger coursed through Maggie. "Why are you doing this to Ina? She's done nothing to you."

"Let's just say I'm improvising. I hadn't planned any of this when I went to her house to look for the thumb drive. Didn't even know she was home. Nobody answered the doorbell or my knocking at either door. Figured she had the drive since I didn't find it at your house." Alex walked from one side of Ina to the other, the knife blade pointing at her prey the whole time. "While she was downstairs frantically looking for someone outside, I shinnied into the open window upstairs. And do you know what I found hanging over the bathtub?"

Maggie's mind flipped through the previous day's events before Ina called her. She remembered the trip to the camera shop and the man who entered the shop and followed them outside. The "man" who was really Alex. "Photos?"

"Yes, photos." Alex's pacing continued. "The moment I saw them, I knew what I had to do. She deserves to die every bit as much as Francesco. Maybe even more."

As Alex's rambling escalated, the door opened several inches, and the woman from the window slipped inside holding a whip in each hand. She held a finger to her lips and inched farther into the room. Maggie focused her eyes on James to keep from looking at and betraying the person she believed was there to save them. His color had returned, and his eyes were more alert.

"I don't know what you think they did, but Francesco didn't deserve to die, and neither does Ina." Maggie spoke with a strength born of knowing help had arrived. Expecting Alex to attack, Maggie scooted back a couple of feet. Instead of advancing on Maggie, however, the knife thrower returned to Ina. Maggie let out a frustrated breath. She'd failed to distract Alex.

Alex continued to rant, the knife still on Ina's neck. She blamed Ina and Marco Cavallo for her grandfather's failures, her father's alcoholism, and her own cursed existence. Still and silent, Ina stared straight ahead. Confused to say the least, Maggie prayed Ina would be able to stay calm.

The long-haired woman inched closer. She cracked her whip and flung it across the room, wrapping the braided leather around

Alex's neck and yanking her to the floor. The knife clattered to the ground. Ina's eyes closed and she breathed deeply.

"That's for my brother, Francesco." The woman's voice was colder than Alex's.

"So you're Gabriella," Alex said with a sneer.

"Our hero," Ina said, her voice strong. "And I do believe she's just taken you down."

Alex's chest rose and fell. Her green eyes blazed. "I don't think so." She sprang to her feet, her free hand hovering over her belt. In a flash, a knife was in her hand and slicing through the whip with such precision she didn't draw a drop of her own blood. The end of the whip fell to the floor.

Maggie's mouth dropped open.

"Your brother—well, he wasn't so smart. He was easy to trace after he went nosing around the circus asking questions about the Cavallo family. The fake last name didn't fool anybody." Alex's eyes grew wild. "He was even easier to kill."

Gabriella retracted her shortened whip and brought it to her side as she cracked her second whip over the woman's head. "Francesco wasn't a threat to you. He was writing a book about our family. He was researching my father's history."

"A threat? Ha. I never saw him as a threat." Alex's voice dripped with sarcasm. "I did a bit of sleuthing on my own. Imagine my glee when I uncovered he was Marco Cavallo's son. What better way to torture the man who ruined my grandfather's career—and my family's destiny—than maiming his only son?"

Gabriella cracked her good whip, then wound it around Alex's body. With a yank, she brought the knife thrower to her knees. "You did more than maim him."

Alex swiftly sprang to her feet, her lips curled into a smile though the whip remained twined around her body. "Did I? Perhaps I did push the knife in rather hard."

"Don't try my patience. I don't have as much of it as my brother did." Gabriella tugged on her whip.

Alex didn't budge. "I must compliment the historical society museum in this town. I followed Francesco and learned a lot of information about the circus while eavesdropping during his conversation with the curator. I asked a few questions of my own after he left. Very knowledgeable woman."

Filled with rage and frustration and emboldened by Gabriella's presence, Maggie slowly stood up and edged closer to Alex. "You broke into my home. Why? I have nothing to do with any of this."

"You had something I wanted."

Maggie began to wrap her mind around the recent craziness. "Francesco's thumb drive."

"Ding ding ding! Give the woman a prize." Alex laughed. "I don't understand people who are so trusting they don't have security alarms in their homes, especially when they contain valuable antiques."

Maggie was losing patience in getting to the truth. "I'd met Francesco minutes before he was killed. How did you know I had the thumb drive? I didn't even know until this morning."

"I guess I'm more observant than you are." Alex's tone was smug despite the whip around her torso. "I saw him slip it into your purse. I was sitting right next to you. I even spoke to your friend the waitress."

Maggie remembered the woman who'd been so rude to Daisy. "Wild red hair and a muumuu." She shook her head. "What was so important about the thumb drive?"

"Ah, so I did make an impression." Alex fixed her gaze on Maggie. "I wanted to see what Francesco was really up to—and to find out information about his father. I really wanted to kill *him*." She grinned. "But Francesco was handier."

Gabriella tensed. Her knuckles on the handle of the whip

whitened. Her nostrils flared. "Francesco was innocent. Your hatred is obviously for my father."

"Ah, but what better way to exact revenge on a father than to kill his beloved son?"

Not wanting to stand between Alex and Gabriella, Maggie stepped out of the line of fire, grabbed her purse, and inched back to James. She was a few feet from him when he stabbed his finger in the direction of Alex's weapon belt. "Look out," he whispered. While Gabriella was overwhelmed with grief and anger about Francesco's murder, Alex's arm stretched out, her hand reaching for her weapons.

Alex's hand inched toward a dagger hanging from her belt. In a flash, she pulled out the dagger, sliced the whip and leaped to her feet. "You're a little rusty, Gabriella. Getting old, are you?"

Maggie looked at both women. She and Gabriella were probably close in age, in their midforties. Alex appeared to be about ten years younger.

Gabriella cracked the shortened whip in her right hand, and the two women crouched and shadowed each other's moves. Maggie held her breath, unnerved by the standoff.

"Older and wiser," Gabriella said, her voice controlled. "Do you know what really happened in the horse tent all those years ago?"

"Yeah, your father and this woman permanently disabled my grandfather."

"Ha." Gabriella's eyes were glued to Alex's face. "Your grandfather was an egotistical brute who believed every woman should swoon in his presence. My grandmother didn't. When she rejected him, he snapped and attacked her."

Alex sucked in a breath. "You liar."

"The truth is your grandfather is hardly a saint."

"Lies! Everyone is lying." She stomped her feet and covered her ears with her hands. "Make them stop, Poppa. You were the Amazing Emil Lupei. Tell them. Command respect, Poppa!"

Gabriella blinked and stood so still Maggie thought she was holding her breath. But she grasped her whips and stood poised to use them. Alex moaned and rocked slightly, her eyes staring straight ahead. Her hands floated down from her face.

Adrenaline pumping, Maggie pulled the pepper spray from her purse and walked toward Alex with the canister outstretched. She pressed down on the button, releasing the spray as Alex's fingertips touched the dagger.

Alex shrieked and covered her eyes with her hands. She rolled on the floor, yelling for her henchmen. Gabriella held her still with a booted foot, unsnapped the weapon belt from Alex's waist, and tossed it toward the wall.

"There's no need to scream," Gabriella said. "I've taken care of your two sidekicks. They're a bit tied up at the moment." She bound Alex's hands together with what remained of the whip in her right hand, her other whip held at the ready in her left hand.

"Yikes, and so is Ina." Maggie shoved the pink canister into her pants pocket and dashed to Alex's belt. She pulled out a knife, went to Ina, and started to cut the rope around her hands.

"Be careful with that knife," Gabriella warned. "It's as sharp as her tongue." She smiled at Maggie and Ina, then looked down at Alex, who was still secured beneath Gabriella's boot. "I should kill you with one of your own knives, a dagger like you used to kill my brother." She shook her head. "But I won't. An eye for an eye is no way to live."

"I think that makes you smart as a whip, dear," Ina quipped.

Ina's snappy words transformed Maggie's pain, frustration,

and fear into an uncontrollable need to laugh as she finished removing Ina's restraints. As Maggie's chuckles bubbled to the surface and morphed into belly laughs, the door to the building crashed open. Police officers in black SWAT team garb swarmed the room. "Freeze! State police!"

18

Maggie's laugh caught in her throat as guns pointed at them from all sides. She threw her hands in the air. The knife clattered to the floor.

"Drop your weapons." The point man trained his pistol on Gabriella.

"Yes sir. I will. I'm Gabriella Valli Stokes. I called 911. This woman is trained in martial arts and she's a knife-throwing expert. I suggest someone grab that weapon belt and move it as far away as you can before I step off of her."

The point man nodded to an officer on the other side of the room and gestured toward Alex's belt. The officer returned the nod, hustled to grab the belt, and returned to his position.

"May I also suggest handcuffing Ms. Lupei before I release my whips? She may only have one working eye thanks to some pepper spray, but she's still a professional escape artist."

The point man nodded to an officer inching along the wall. Maggie was relieved to see the familiar face of Robert Linton among the sea of black uniforms. When he reached Ina and Maggie, Officer Linton picked up the knife Maggie had dropped, then squatted in front of his aunt's chair. He gently touched the black-and-blue bruises around her lips where she'd been gagged. Without speaking, he pushed up the sleeves of her shirt and studied the burn marks left by the ropes. "Thank God you're all right," he said. "You gave me a few gray hairs today."

"Ah, they'll make you look more distinguished." Ina grinned. "But that doesn't mean you can lose your boyish charm."

"Never, Aunt Ina." He raised his eyes to Maggie. "You've been through the wringer this week too. Are you all right?"

"I'm tired and achy, but fine. A good night of sleep and I'll be as good as new."

Officer Linton stood up and pulled Ina to her feet. "You two are the strongest women I know. I wouldn't want to be on the wrong end of one of your mysteries, especially now that I know your skills in crime board creation."

Across the room, Officer Crosby questioned James, who was not only standing but had regained normal color in his face.

The reunions were cut short when Alex began hurling insults at the officers handcuffing her. "You'll never get away with this," she growled as an officer pulled her arms behind her back to snap handcuffs on her wrists. "You idiots! I'm not the one you should arrest!" Alex, arms held on each side by officers, twisted around and glared at Ina. "You should be arresting her! She destroyed my grandfather!"

The stern-faced officers dragged her kicking and screaming out the door.

"You'll regret this, I promise you! Take your hands off me or you'll be sorry—"

She was still hollering as the door of the patrol car closed. Its siren wailed as it pulled away.

"Aunt Ina, your throat has a cut." Robert Linton lifted his aunt's chin with care. "The paramedics should take a look at this. The ambulance is right outside."

"Don't be silly. I'm fine." Ina patted his cheek. "Nothing a little bandage and peroxide won't heal. I can take care of that myself. Besides, I might miss something if I'm stuck in an ambulance."

"What about you, Maggie?" Robert gave her a concerned look. "Looks like she got you too."

Maggie shook her head. "Ditto what Ina said. Let's get to the station."

Officer Crosby, James, and the point man crossed the room. "This is Lieutenant Yamada of the Maine State Police," Officer Crosby said. "Lieutenant, this is Maggie Watson and Ina Linton, Robert's aunt."

"And I'm Curtis Etling, reporter for the *New York Examiner.*" Curtis strode into the room. "I was heading back to the hotel when I saw police vehicles zipping by. Thought I should check it out. Reporter's intuition. One of the officers outside said I might be able to get a comment after the witnesses were interviewed."

James bristled. "Etling, this isn't the time or place—"

Maggie rested a hand on his arm. "James, it's okay. Curtis was Francesco's friend."

"Curtis!" Gabriella ran toward the reporter, hugging him warmly.

"Hey, Gabby. Long time no see."

Maggie watched Francesco's sister and best friend reunite, their embrace charged with grief, and wishing they were seeing each other again under very different circumstances.

James allowed them a few moments, then spoke up. "I suggest we go to the police station, where we'd be more comfortable." He cut his eyes toward the reporter. "You too, Etling."

Robert eyed Lieutenant Yamada. "You okay with that?"

The lieutenant nodded. "I'll meet you at the station as soon as the crime scene unit arrives. We'll talk to the reporter after we finish the questioning."

"Sounds good. Thank you." Curtis checked his watch and started for the door. "I'll meet you there. I need to give my editor a call." He saluted the police officers and jogged out of the room.

"I'll drive Aunt Ina to the station." Robert looked across the room to where Gabriella was studying the weaponry Alex left behind. "Mrs. Stokes, do you need a ride too?"

"No thanks. I hid my car in the cemetery." Gabriella eyeballed her whips. "I don't suppose I can take them with me?"

"Afraid not," Yamada said. "Not now, anyway. Crime scene techs are on their way."

"I understand," Gabriella said, turning to face Officer Linton. "I parked my rental car on the other side of the mausoleum at the border of the cemetery. I'll drive to the station."

"I'd prefer to escort you, ma'am," Officer Linton said. "We can drive you back to your car after we talk at the station."

Gabriella nodded, then she, Maggie, James, and Ina followed Officer Linton to the door of the depot, leaving Lieutenant Yamada and his team inside. As they crossed the threshold, a deafening crash from the cemetery reverberated across the old railroad yard, and a cloud of smoke wafted into the air.

"What in the world?" Lieutenant Yamada appeared in the doorway. He squinted, gazing toward the smoke. "It's the cruiser. It plowed into a mausoleum."

He signaled his team and turned to Officers Linton and Crosby. "Take the witnesses to the police station for questioning." Yamada yanked the radio from his belt. "I'll call it in. Get these people out of here."

Robert nodded. Yamada joined the SWAT team as it entered the field and crept across the field in a snakelike line.

James stared at the police cruiser. "All of us won't fit. My car is by the road, quite a distance from the cemetery. I'm feeling better. I'll head to my car and meet you at the police station."

Officers Linton and Crosby exchanged glances. "I'll go with Alderman Bennett," Officer Crosby said. "I can check the vehicle and ride with him to ensure he reaches the station safely."

"Works for me," James said. He and Officer Crosby took off toward his car.

After Maggie retrieved her phone from where she'd dropped

it outside, she joined Ina and Gabriella in Robert's car as the crime scene van and two more cruisers pulled up to the old depot building. Robert watched the new arrivals open their vehicle doors. "I'll be right back. I'm just going to update them."

Silence filled the car. Maggie guessed the other women were processing what had happened just as she was. Exhausted, she pressed her nose to the window and watched the snaking line of police officers disappear into the shallow valley between the depot and the edge of the cemetery.

. . . .

Maggie blinked and gazed at the clock on the wall of the interrogation room at the Somerset Harbor Police Station. *Two p.m.?* She'd lost track of time that morning, watching Alex rant and threaten them with weapons in the old depot building.

Ina, Maggie, James, and Gabriella sat on one side of a long table. Officers Williams and Crosby faced them. Robert Linton, unable to participate in the questioning because of his relationship to Ina, sat on the end next to his aunt.

Officer Williams stroked his mustache as he rifled through the sheets of paper in front of him. "Ms. Linton, walk us through what happened to you yesterday afternoon."

Ina cleared her throat. "I'd just finished developing some photo negatives in the upstairs bathroom when the doorbell rang. When I went downstairs and opened the door, nobody was there."

Williams scribbled on his paper. "Then what happened?"

"A couple of minutes later, someone pounded on my back door." Ina blew out a breath. "This went on two or three more times. It was spooky, so I called Maggie and told her to come over."

"And then?"

"I went upstairs to my bedroom and locked the door to wait

for Maggie." Ina's fingers tapped the table. "I sat on the bed and stared at the bedroom door, waiting for the doorbell to ring."

"Did the doorbell ring?"

"No. I was grabbed from behind and gagged. It was Alex. She came in through the open window." Ina smirked. "She tried to hog-tie me, even put a knife to my throat, but I fought like crazy. She had my arms, but I kicked with all I had."

"We noticed the trail of toppled furniture," Officer Crosby said, flashing a brief smile.

"She muscled me out the front door and into her SUV without a single neighbor seeing us."

Officer Williams rubbed a hand over his stubby crew cut. "Where did she take you?"

"Straight to the old depot near the old circus grounds."

He leaned forward and put his elbows on the table. "Why did she take you from your home?"

Ina lifted her chin. "She was ranting something about me ruining her grandfather's life. I didn't understand." Ina paused and bit her lip. "She said Maggie and I would have to die because we saw her outside The Busy Bean after she killed Francesco."

"Why did she kill him?"

"I don't know." Ina cut her eyes to Gabriella. "It sounded like she was avenging what had been done to her family over sixty years ago."

"Mrs. Stokes." Officer Williams shifted his gaze to Gabriella. "Why was your brother in Somerset Harbor?"

Gabriella perched on the edge of her seat. "My brother was writing a book about my father. He came here, I think, to chase down a family mystery, a question my father would never answer."

"Who's your father?"

"Marc Valli."

"Marc Valli is your father? *Turbo Drive* is my favorite movie!

Man, that scene where he jumps from one semi to the other? Incredible!" Officer Williams nearly bounced with excitement in his chair before calming himself.

"He'd be happy to know it." Apparently noticing everyone else's questioning expressions, Gabriella explained, "He's a well-respected Hollywood stuntman, and he even starred in a few action movies in the 1970s. He retired about ten years ago, although he still consults on films from time to time." She brushed a lock of brunette hair out of her face. "He and my grandmother, Lia Cavallo, were circus performers until they fled in the 1950s. Why they left is a mystery. They changed their last name from Cavallo to Valli and refused to talk about family history before they arrived in Hollywood, no matter how many times we asked. Grandmother took the story to her grave." Gabriella's eyes filled with tears. "Francesco was obsessed with finding out why they left the circus. He wanted to include it in my father's biography."

Officer Crosby cleared her throat. "You're saying it's not a coincidence he showed up in Somerset Harbor around the same time as the Circus de Vita?"

"After this morning I'm convinced it isn't. He came here looking for this particular circus in this specific town. He was chasing a lead." Gabriella looked at Maggie. "I know you and Ms. Linton were the last people to talk with Francesco. What did he say?"

"We didn't talk long. He said he was researching a book. He mentioned the circus and said many Hollywood stars began their careers under the big top."

"Ms. Linton," Gabriella said, turning to Ina, "do you remember anything else about your conversation with my brother?"

"Not a thing." Ina drummed her fingers on the table. "Maggie pretty much covered it."

The conversation was interrupted by a knock on the inter-rogation room door. Officer Williams excused himself and left the room. His face was ashen when he returned two minutes later. "Alex Lupei has escaped." He looked at Gabriella. "In your rental car."

19

Maggie and Ina gasped and stared at each other with wide eyes. "So this isn't over," Maggie said, her stomach churning.

"Don't worry, Robert will take care of us," Ina said with a confidence Maggie couldn't quite muster. "Right, Robert?"

"Right." His look was grim. "I won't let anything happen to you."

James squeezed Maggie's hand. "We'll get through this, I promise."

"Alderman Bennett," Officer Williams said, "Chief Cole said to let you know he'll be in to bring us up to date in a few minutes."

"Good." James released Maggie's hand. "I assume he has a plan to protect witnesses."

"Yes sir," Officer Williams said, then checked the wall clock. "It might be a few minutes. Can I get anyone coffee or water?"

"I could use some coffee." Maggie leaned toward a peaked Ina. "How about you? Have you had anything to eat or drink since yesterday afternoon?"

"A little water."

"Ina! Why didn't you say something?"

"We've had other things to deal with than my stomach. Like surviving."

"I'll see what I can round up for you," Officer Williams said. "Can't have you fainting on our watch."

The room was silent as Officer Williams walked to the door. When it closed behind him, Officer Crosby pushed her chair back. "This might be a good time to stand up and stretch your legs or use the restroom."

Overcome with fatigue, Maggie crossed her arms on the table and laid her head on them. Her eyes fluttered shut as chairs scraped on the floor around her. Officer Crosby escorted Ina and Gabriella to the restroom. Officer Williams returned with a few cups of coffee, then he and James paced around the room in whispered conversation. Maggie willed her mind to shut down and give her peace, if only for a couple of minutes.

. . . .

"Maggie, wake up," James whispered, tapping her arm. "Chief Cole and Lieutenant Yamada are here."

She fought through the fog in her head. "Chief Cole?" Maggie sat up, rubbing her eyes. When they focused, she was thankful to see a to-go cup of coffee in front of her. "How long was I asleep?"

"About ten minutes. You needed it."

Next to her, Ina munched on vending machine peanut butter crackers and sipped a canned soda. Gabriella and the police officers had returned to their places at the table. Chief Cole and a stone-faced Lieutenant Yamada stood behind the seated officers.

"I commend everyone in this room for their actions today." Chief Cole, his face haggard under his thinning salt-and-pepper hair, made eye contact with each person sitting around the table. "But despite the bravery of all involved, the suspect Alex Lupei escaped custody at approximately thirteen hundred hours. Lupei had hidden a smoke bomb on her person and detonated it inside the police cruiser as two Maine State Police officers drove toward the cemetery access road. The driver evidently became disoriented in the smoke and fumes and lost control of the cruiser. The vehicle came to a stop when it crashed into a mausoleum at the edge of the cemetery. When the smoke cleared, Lupei was gone, and the handcuffs were found in the back seat. Both officers are at the hospital being treated for minor injuries."

Maggie put a hand on Ina's and squeezed. Their eyes met, horror on their faces.

Chief Cole took a breath. "Given Lupei's extraordinary abilities, she's considered armed and dangerous. The department will provide protection until she's apprehended. I thought you should know before the press has time to get the story out. Any questions?"

Yeah, when is this craziness going to stop? Maggie kept the thought to herself. "When will I be able to go home?"

"We're working out the details and will let you know soon." The chief shifted his weight. "Right now, there's a reporter outside the room, Curtis Etling, who says he's been promised the story. Is he telling the truth?"

"Yes, Curtis deserves this story," Maggie said. "Francesco was his friend and colleague. He wants the truth to come out as much as we do."

Chief Cole turned to his officers. "You okay with this?"

"Yeah," Crosby and Linton said in unison.

"Then it's okay with me."

"One more thing, sir." Robert stood straighter. "My partner and I would like to keep an eye on my aunt and Mrs. Watson if that's okay."

"Fine. Keep me posted." The chief strode to the door and opened it. Curtis appeared in the doorway. "Seems you've got yourself a scoop, Etling."

The reporter approached Chief Cole and extended his hand. "Thank you, sir."

"You're welcome," the chief said, shaking the proffered hand. "You can thank Mrs. Watson for speaking up and these officers for giving the okay. Perhaps you'll have something to add to the investigation, given your contact with Francesco Valli."

"I appreciate it." Curtis entered the room.

"Lieutenant, you're welcome to stay for the questioning," Chief Cole said.

"No thank you," Yamada said. "I need to check on my men. I'll read the report after it's filed."

As Chief Cole and Lieutenant Yamada closed the door behind them, Curtis took a seat at the opposite end of the table from Robert, set a notepad on the table, and took out a pen.

Maggie took a sip of coffee. "Curtis, before you get started, may I ask a question of anyone here who may be able to answer it?"

"Go ahead."

She looked around the table and cleared her throat. "Why did Gabriella and Ina seem so surprised when Alex said Emil Lupei was alive?"

Ina cleared her throat. "Because we both thought I'd killed him."

20

Robert took his aunt's hand as stunned faces turned in her direction. "Aunt Ina, do you know what you're saying?"

"Yes, Robert. I do." Ina removed her hand from her nephew's grasp. "I suppose I've kept this secret long enough."

"Go on." Officer Linton put a protective arm across the back of her chair.

"A long time ago, when I was about thirteen years old, my parents, my brother, Wallace, and I went to see the circus here in Somerset Harbor. It was our annual tradition." She smiled. "I loved the circus, and I was particularly excited that year, even though Hattie, my best friend, wouldn't be able to go with me. She was sick."

"Why were you more excited than usual?" Officer Williams asked.

"I'd been given a box camera for Christmas, and I loved it as much as I love the circus. I couldn't wait to get to the big top and take photos." Her eyes twinkled. "Everyone said I had a flair for photography." She paused and sipped her soda. "Mother and Father indulged my habit and gave me freedom to explore as long as I was back in my seat before the show started. You see, as much as I loved the daring stunts and glittery costumes, what fascinated me was the activity and people behind the scenes. I wandered around looking in the railroad cars, tents, and animal cages, taking photo after photo. Nobody paid me any mind."

Officer Williams tapped his pen on the table. "Did something happen while you were looking around?"

"I peeked into the horse tent. The horses were restless, so I stepped inside and started snapping photos of the horses and equipment in the tent. Then I discovered why they were snorting and stamping their hooves."

"And why were the horses upset?"

"Keep in mind I was only thirteen years old." Ina closed her eyes a moment and took a deep breath before opening them. "When I walked into the tent, a man was attacking a woman, and a boy was trying to pull him away from her. The man was practically snarling. His eyes were wild. It looked like he was hurting the woman and was going to harm the boy."

Ina sat back in her chair and rubbed her temples.

"And then what?" Gabriella, who had been quiet for quite some time, finally piped up. "We need to hear the rest."

"It was awful. I was mad at the man for what he was doing, and I was scared. I took a picture of what was happening, but I threw my camera on the ground when the man reached out and grabbed the boy by the throat. And then I—"

Ina buried her face in her hands and shook all over.

"Aunt Ina?" Robert put his hand on her back to comfort her.

She raised her head. "I'm sorry. I was afraid he was going to kill the woman and the boy. I reached for the first thing I could find—a shovel. I hit him on the back of the head and he crumpled to the dirt." Ina's eyes filled with tears. "He didn't move after that."

Everyone in the room sat in stunned silence for a few moments.

Ina cleared her throat and wiped her eyes with the back of her hands. Her eyes on Gabriella, she said, "The woman, your grandmother, staggered to her feet and hugged me. She thanked me for saving her life and her son's life. Then she took me by the shoulders and told me to run and find my parents. She told me to blend in with the crowd and leave the circus as soon as I could without causing a fuss."

Ina's hands were shaking, a sight Maggie had never seen. Maggie covered the trembling hands with her own fingers. "You can do this," she said. "Tell us the rest."

"Gabriella's grandmother said to never speak of that day again. She promised to take care of everything else and then disappear." Ina leaned forward and turned her head toward Gabriella. "I was so scared I did what I was told and kept it all a secret. I checked the newspaper for months looking for an article about the killing or maiming of a circus performer, but I never saw one."

"It doesn't surprise me," Gabriella said. "In those days, the circus took care of its own issues and rarely contacted local law enforcement when its people were killed or injured. That's probably why my grandmother instructed you as she did. Circus vengeance could be more treacherous than the law. I think Alex and her misguided vendetta against you and my father and grandmother gives an idea of the danger."

"What happened to the photos you took?" Officer Williams broke in with his own questions.

"I gave the film to my friend Hattie and asked her to keep it in a safe place with the circus program and poster. I didn't see any of those things until Hattie's daughter returned them to me earlier this week. I never expected to see them again. I didn't want to." Ina met Officer Williams's gaze. "I never quite got over killing that man. It's haunted me for over sixty years. That's why I was shocked to find out Emil Lupei was alive. Shocked and relieved."

Questions bounced around Maggie's brain. She could only imagine what Ina was thinking and feeling. "No wonder you weren't acting like yourself. It took a lot of courage to develop that film."

"It was difficult, but I'm glad I did. I had to face my past." Ina shifted in her seat. "Alex noticed the prints hanging up to dry in the bathroom as she was forcing me out of the house. She practically roared when she saw the one of her grandfather assaulting Lia. She tore them down in a rage and brought them along."

"Speaking of Lia," Maggie said, "Gabriella, what happened to your father and grandmother?"

"It's quite a story, which is why Francesco was going to write a book about it." Gabriella's face became animated. "When my father, then known as Marco Cavallo, and my grandmother, Lia Cavallo, fled the circus, they made their way across the country to California. They took odd jobs in towns along the way, staying in each one until they had enough money to move on."

Curtis, who'd been scribbling silently, gazed at Gabriella as if seeing her for the first time. "What happened when they arrived in California? I knew Francesco for over twenty years. He never said a word about any of this."

Gabriella bit her lip. "He didn't know any of it." Tears welled in her eyes. "Grandmother died a few years ago, and Dad didn't tell me the story until after Francesco was murdered. I think he knew his past had caught up with him. In retrospect, I realize he was never too keen on my brother writing the book."

"What happened when they arrived in California?"

"My father and grandmother used the skills they honed in the circus to find work performing stunts for the film industry. Dad changed his name to Marc Valli and became one of the most sought-after and celebrated stuntmen in the industry."

"And starred in the best movie of 1975," Officer Williams said, then blushed a bit at his uncharacteristically enthusiastic outburst.

"Yes, he did. Though after that, he decided he preferred to fly a little more under the radar." Gabriella smiled, then turned to Curtis. "May I borrow your cell phone?" After the reporter handed her his smartphone, she opened the browser and typed a few keywords into a search, then passed it back. "Grandmother was no slouch either. She was one of the first women to have a stunt career in Hollywood. When Francesco and I were little, she took us to movie sets so we could see how stunt doubles work. Here she is in the '60s, standing on one foot on a moving motorcycle, riding around a studio lot."

Curtis studied the photo. "I'll bet she had some tales to tell."

"That's an understatement. Her stories drew me into stunt work, although these days I mostly run a variety of stunt-based fitness classes at my studio in New York." Gabriella stretched her long arms gracefully. "Francesco and I were both trained in stunt work."

Curtis sat back and whistled. "That's quite a story." He shook his head. "I still can't believe he kept it from me."

"He didn't know the entire story, like I said. My grandmother slipped up one day years ago and mentioned working in the circus. She played dumb when we asked questions. We only knew they'd left the circus and wouldn't talk about it. We didn't know why."

"What happened to your grandmother?"

"Grandmother was a legend in her own right. She died in her sleep after a day of training stuntwomen, which was what she loved." Gabriella smiled. "She was eighty-four."

She pushed her chair from the table, walked over to Ina, and knelt beside her. "You remind me of my grandmother. You have the same spirit." Gabriella braced herself with one hand on the table. "Now that I've found you, I know my father will want to thank the girl who saved his family. Are you up for a trip to New York City?"

Ina studied Gabriella's face for several seconds and nodded. "I want to meet your father, so we can both put this behind us. But I wonder—what has become of Emil Lupei?"

"During her rant, Alex said he lives in New York City. I

have connections who can find him for us. We'll go see him too if you'd like."

Ina stared ahead and seemed a million miles away. Finally, she looked at Maggie. "What do you say we go to New York on an adventure?"

"I think it's your call, Ina, but I'm game if you are." Maggie reached for her purse and pulled out her phone. "Speaking of call, my phone rang at the vigil, and I never did answer it." She punched in her voice mail code and listened to the message. "It was the curator of the circus museum. He gave me the year the poster was published and the names of the headliners pictured on it. But now I understand why you reacted so strongly to the poster: Emil Lupei and Lia Cavallo were featured. Lia was the dancer standing on the horse's back, and Emil was one of the trapeze artists in a spotlight. They were the stars of the show."

"I'd say the curator was a day late and a dollar short with that information," Ina said, the old spark returning to her eyes.

Officer Williams stood up. "I think we're done here. Etling, you got all you need?"

The reporter nodded. "Thank you."

The group filed out of the interrogation room and walked down the hallway to the lobby. As they crossed the lobby, a camera crew burst through the glass door. Maggie recognized the same anchor who had been at the vigil, and Juliet was close on his heels.

Maggie seized Curtis's arm. "Why were you talking with Juliet outside the printshop?"

"Juliet?" He followed Maggie's gaze to the commotion across the lobby. "Oh, you mean the barracuda?" He chuckled. "I asked her for directions to The Busy Bean. I wanted to see if anyone there had seen Francesco. She went into full flirt mode."

"Why did she point at me?"

He smiled. "I asked if she knew the lady who owned the antiques shop. I didn't tell her I was working on a news story. She wasn't amused I asked about you."

James chuckled. "Judging by the attention she's giving that news anchor, she has shifted her attentions elsewhere."

Curtis shook his head. "Poor guy."

"Juliet's not so bad, but she's not my type," James said. "Maggie, I confronted Juliet about the text you received canceling our lunch. After I made it clear I wasn't interested in her romantically, she confessed to sending it and then deleting the evidence. You were right about needing a security code for my cell phone." He plucked up her hand and placed it in the crook of his arm. "Now, how about that alarm system for Sedgwick Manor?"

Before Maggie could reply, Curtis tapped her shoulder. "Don't look now, but here she comes."

"Oh, James, there you are." Juliet scurried up in her five-inch heels. "I'll see you bright and early tomorrow at the Witmarsh Mansion, right? I want to present the outdoor kitchen and landscaping plans based on the pieces from Maggie's shop."

"I'll be there," James replied. He turned to talk to Curtis.

Juliet tugged on Maggie's arm, pulling her away from the group. "You're a lucky woman. James truly cares for you."

Maggie didn't want to have this conversation with Juliet. "We're just friends, really."

"I beg to differ." Juliet's mouth curved into what seemed like a genuine smile. "He totally ignored all of my advances, and men don't do that. It's obvious he has feelings for you."

"We're friends," Maggie repeated.

"If you say so. Look, I don't apologize often, but I'm sorry for sending the text canceling your lunch with him."

Maggie stared at Juliet. "Why did you do it?"

Juliet glanced down, then met Maggie's gaze again. "He left

his phone on his office desk when he went to get his briefcase from his car. I thought it was the perfect opportunity to get rid of the competition. But I know now I never had a chance with James."

"Oh" was all Maggie could think of to say.

Juliet grinned and held her hand out to Maggie. "I'll keep Carriage House Antiques in mind for future projects. It's a fabulous shop." Juliet walked away but turned around after three paces. "Just one word of advice: Open your eyes, Maggie Watson." Juliet spun on her stilettos and made a beeline to her newest love interest, who welcomed her with matched enthusiasm.

Reeling, Maggie returned to the group, and they all left the building together—two cops, two good friends, a reporter, a stuntwoman, and James, the one she couldn't quite label, despite her protestations to Juliet. The sun was sinking in the sky. Maggie breathed in the cool air. "What a day."

She came to a dead stop in the middle of the parking lot. "Where on earth are we going? I don't have a car here."

"You and Aunt Ina are riding in the patrol car with Crosby and me. No discussion." Robert Linton crossed his arms. "And Crosby and I are going to stay with both of you until Alex is caught or you take off for New York with Gabriella. We doubt she'll leave the area now that she knows you're here, but we'll notify the authorities in New York to be on the lookout in case she does try to follow you."

"I suppose I could use some quality time with my favorite nephew," Ina said.

"I was hoping you'd agree without a fuss." Robert's face relaxed. "I think all of you would be safest at Sedgwick Manor with Crosby and me on watch."

"Thanks, but I need to get back to my hotel and work on this story for the paper. My editor has already left nine messages."

Curtis waved his notebook in the air. "But I could use a lift. I walked to the old train depot since it's so close."

"I'll give you a ride," James offered. "My car is here." James hugged Maggie and released her before she could say anything. "I'll stay in contact with you. Let me know your plans."

Gabriella cleared her throat. "Curtis, are you headed back to New York too? I'd like for you to come along to see my father, if possible." Her eyes filled with tears. "You were Francesco's friend. Papa would like to see you."

"I haven't seen your father in a long time. Francesco and I used to go to his place to watch the Jets play when he first moved to New York. It tapered off when the newspaper cut its staff and we all had to work longer hours." He rubbed the corner of one eye. "It would be great to see him again. I'll check with my editor and let you know."

"I'll count on you. Call Maggie in the morning for our travel details."

"What about you? Where are you staying?" Maggie asked Gabriella as James and Curtis started across the parking lot.

"Don't worry about me. I have a safe place to stay. I'll make arrangements for our flights to New York, and then I'll be in touch." She hugged Ina and Maggie. "My father will be surprised."

Gabriella disappeared among the lengthening shadows as the sun began its descent.

The sky was beginning to lighten the next morning as Robert Linton drove his off-duty Ford Explorer past the circus grounds on the way out of town. He was taking Ina, Maggie, and Gabriella to the Portland airport for their flight to New York. Curtis, whose editor had asked him to come back to the city to finish his story, was meeting them in the terminal after returning his rental car.

Ina, sitting in the front seat next to her nephew, leaned her forehead against the passenger-side window as they passed the circus's *Welcome* sign and arched gate.

Robert glanced at her. "Aunt Ina, are you okay?"

She turned a bright smiled on him. "I'm better than okay. It's the first time since 1955 that the opening of the circus hasn't filled me with dread."

Maggie reached up and squeezed her friend's shoulder. "I'm glad you don't have a secret hanging over you anymore."

"Me too," Ina said, patting Maggie's hand on her shoulder.

A minute later, Maggie cringed in the back seat as they passed the cemetery and then the berm that hid the old depot. *Will the memory of the cold steel blade pressing against my neck ever fade?* The access road leading into the cemetery where the police cruiser crashed into the mausoleum was still sealed off with yellow-and-black police tape.

"By the way, Lieutenant Yamada called me earlier," Robert said. "Gabriella, he told me your rental car was found abandoned in a wooded area north of town. It's been impounded by the state police. They'll square it with the rental car company." He glanced back at Maggie in the rearview mirror. "Unfortunately, there was no sign of Alex."

Maggie looked away from the window and met Robert's eyes in the mirror. "Do you suppose Alex will follow us to New York?"

"Don't know," Gabriella said, tapping her thigh to the beat of the pop song playing on the radio. "I'm not worried about Alex. I can take her."

Robert eyed her in the rearview mirror. "I can't decide if I find that comforting or disturbing."

"That's because you didn't see her with her whips." Ina gave him a playful slap on the shoulder. "Have a little faith."

"A whip, huh?" Robert arched an eyebrow. "That's a . . . unique talent."

. . . .

A few hours later, Gabriella merged from the airport access road onto a busy highway in New York without blinking an eye as cars zoomed past her compact car. "We have about a half-hour drive from here, depending on the traffic." She peered into the rearview mirror. "I think it's wise to go see Emil Lupei first. Ina can get their reunion of sorts out of the way. Plus, there's a chance he might know where Alex is, and that would be good information to have."

Ina drummed her fingers on the armrest between her and Maggie. "I can't believe your contact was able to find him."

"Zach may be a private investigator now, but in his younger days, he was a circus performer-turned-stuntman, much like my father. Except Zach didn't change his identity." Gabriella turned on her blinker and zoomed into the next lane. "He still has contacts in the circus realm, thank goodness."

Curtis pulled his notepad and pen from the backpack he

had at his feet. "Thanks for letting me tag along and get the rest of the story." He scratched his pen across the pad. "My readers will love the background info."

"Francesco would have wanted you to have the story." Gabriella turned her head to Curtis. "The entire story."

Maggie leaned forward. "Tell us more about Francesco."

Gabriella, two years her brother's senior, regaled them with tales of Francesco's talent for stunts as a kid: walking across the handrail of a river bridge at eight years old, rolling down a hill in a barrel and crashing it to pieces against a tree at twelve, leaping from second-story balconies at sixteen. Neighborhood kids had called him Frankie, like the singer, but Gabriella had insisted on calling him Goober. "Just because it bugged him."

"When did he decide to trade stunt work for journalism?"

"That was my doing." Curtis raised his hand. "We were roommates our freshman year and he hadn't declared a major. I was majoring in journalism and working on the university paper. He caught the bug the day he tagged along with me to cover a student demonstration protesting the use of animals for product testing. He was a natural."

"I'd say so since he won a Pulitzer," Maggie said. "I read that he was a fearless bulldog as a journalist, but the man Ina and I met at The Busy Bean was nervous and fidgety."

"The story he was investigating was personal for Francesco, and for Alex. That's always a game-changer," Curtis explained. "But make no mistake, Francesco was one of the finest journalists in the world: tenacious, thorough, and accurate. It's just a shame that the story he was chasing ended up chasing him."

As the minutes ticked by, everyone in the car grew quieter. When Gabriella pulled into the pleasant, fall-flower-lined entrance to Sunset Garden Nursing Home, Ina grabbed Maggie's arm and squeezed.

Maggie squelched a yelp as Ina squeezed her arm more tightly. "Ina, are you sure you want to do this?"

Ina's gaze was steely. "I have to."

"I think it's best if I do the introductions," Curtis said. "I'm the only one who hasn't tangled with Alex, and maybe I can use my reporter's credentials to smooth things over."

The quartet strolled up a sidewalk lined with marigolds, chrysanthemums, and sweet autumn clematis. Maggie, enjoying the crisp dry air and the sun on her face, slipped her arm through Ina's as they walked up to a set of white double doors under the portico. Curtis held the door for his companions. Inside, he led them to the reception desk.

"We're here to see Emil Lupei." Curtis smiled at the young blonde woman manning the guest log.

"Sign in, please." She returned his smile. "Do you know where you're going?"

Before Curtis could answer, Gabriella stepped forward. "He's in room 222."

"Take the first right, then turn left at the nurse's station." The receptionist handed each of them a *Visitor* sticker.

Curtis eyed her name tag. "Thank you, Melissa. You've been most helpful."

"Glad you had the room number," Curtis said to Gabriella as they took the first turn. "The PI get that for you?"

"He did. Zach doesn't forget small details."

"I might ask you for his number. Never know when you'll need a good private eye."

They took a left at the nurse's station and found Emil's room halfway down the hall on the left, but the door was closed. Curtis tapped on it.

"Mr. Lupei is in the garden," a nurse's aide with a pronounced New York accent said. "He always goes to the garden after lunch."

Maggie scanned the walls for a sign pointing to the garden. "How do we get there from here?"

The aide gestured down the hallway. "Head left at the end of this corridor and you'll see the doors." She smiled. "I'm glad you're visiting. Mr. Lupei doesn't get many visitors these days except his granddaughter."

"Oh, does Alex come to visit often?" Maggie tried to sound casual.

"Usually once or twice a week, but I haven't seen her in almost a month."

"Thank you for your help." Curtis took Maggie's elbow and started down the hallway, Gabriella and Ina trailing behind them. "You have guts, but your delivery was a little stilted."

Ina thumped him on the arm. "Hey, she got us some information, didn't she?"

"She did." He rubbed the spot Ina had hit. "I'll grant her that."

They turned the corner and saw a set of French doors. Curtis opened one and moved aside. "After you, ladies."

They took a few steps down a ramp onto a patio filled with round tables topped with umbrellas to shade the sun. Potted plants surrounded the area. On the far side of the patio, another ramp led to a sidewalk meandering through a walled garden.

"What a lovely place to get fresh air," Maggie said, snaking her way through the tables to the edge of the patio. A lone figure in a wheelchair sat next to a bed of flowers identical to those along the building's entrance. "That must be Emil Lupei."

"He doesn't look quite as menacing as I remember," Ina whispered, her gaze glued to the man in the wheelchair. "Time does take its toll."

"Are you ready for this?" Curtis's eyes softened. "Facing Emil Lupei won't be easy for any of you."

Ina lifted her chin. "I'm ready."

Curtis held his arm out for Ina to grasp. "We can do this."

"Yes we can." Gabriella fell in behind them next to Maggie. "You're a good friend to take this journey with Ina, Maggie. I'm glad you're here."

"Me too." Maggie watched Ina marching with her head held high and her back straight. Even still, Curtis's tall frame dwarfed her. Maggie's heart filled with affection and respect for her friend. "She deserves it. Ina's one of the strongest, most caring people I know."

Curtis slowed his gait as they approached Emil Lupei. He looked back at Maggie and Gabriella for a second and then guided Ina to the wheelchair. Curtis bent over the frail man. "Mr. Lupei?"

Dark eyes under thin gray brows peered up at him. "Do I know you?" His voice was raspy, his legs covered with a colorful blanket.

"No sir, not yet." Curtis squatted beside the wheelchair. "I'm Curtis Etling. This is my friend, Ina Linton." He put one knee on the ground to brace himself. "Mr. Lupei, the only time you and Ina met was over sixty years ago in the horse tent at the Circus de Vita in Somerset Harbor, Maine. She was a young girl who stumbled into the tent to take photos. Do you remember?"

The old man nodded and lifted his eyes to Ina. "You."

"*You*," Ina retorted. "I found out you were alive and thought I'd come see you for myself. All these years, I thought I'd killed you." Ina placed a hand on Curtis's shoulder to steady herself. Her fingers were stark against the dark blue of his shirt. "I didn't mean to hurt anybody in that tent. I was a scared young girl and reacted to what I saw. I heard screams and saw a woman and boy being beaten. I believed I had to do something and jumped in and grabbed the shovel without thinking."

Emil's lips trembled. He appeared to be finding the right words to say. "I'm so sorry for the way I treated Lia Cavallo.

My ego was as large as the big top, and Lia had rejected all my advances. I wasn't accustomed to being told no, and I just snapped one day." His fingers clutched the blanket. "I never saw Lia or her son again. They vanished."

Curtis stood up and drew Gabriella and Maggie into the group. "This is Gabriella Valli Stokes, Lia's granddaughter, and this is Ina's friend, Maggie Watson."

Emil reached his gnarled hands to Gabriella and grasped hers. "A day hasn't gone by that I haven't regretted attacking Lia. I'm so ashamed, but I mended my ways. No more drinking, fighting, or hurting women."

"Grandmother was a very compassionate woman. I'm sure she forgave you a long time ago." Gabriella squeezed his hands. "In fact, she never told any of us what happened. It wasn't until my brother started working on my father's biography that we started nosing around in our family's history with the circus."

"She had a happy life?"

Gabriella nodded. "Long and happy. Grandmother was a pioneer stuntwoman in Hollywood. She was eighty-four years old when she died after a full day of doing what she loved. Her heart simply stopped beating while she was sleeping."

"Means a lot to me to know she had a good life." His eyes misted. "I'm glad I didn't ruin it."

The conversation lulled. Ina's eyes searched Gabriella's. When she didn't speak, Ina moved closer to the wheelchair. "Mr. Lupei, Alex found me this week and accused me of ruining your life. What did she mean?"

"She's bitter because our family never again reached star status." Emil released Gabriella's hands and raised his eyes to Ina's. "After I was hit on the head with the shovel, I developed vertigo and had to give up the trapeze."

"What did you do?"

"I ran the ticket booth. Not nearly as exciting or highly regarded as being a trapeze artist." He shrugged. "But what happened to me made me a better man. I learned to control my temper and respect people. And myself."

Ina patted him on the shoulder. "Huge accomplishments, Mr. Lupei."

"I owe them to you. My biggest regret is I wasn't able to apologize to Lia and ask for forgiveness. By the time I regained consciousness, she and the kid were long gone."

"I'm sure she knew you regretted your actions." Gabriella squeezed his hands. "She was a strong, independent woman with a huge heart."

Sensing Emil's growing fatigue, Maggie broached the question she'd been waiting to ask. "Mr. Lupei, do you know where Alex is now?"

"I don't know, but be careful if you're looking for her. Alex blames everyone but me for what happened in that tent. She got a mean streak from me, and it's bigger than mine ever was."

. . . .

"Uh-oh," Gabriella said, wedging her car into a tiny space behind a commercial van with *Film Crew* scrawled on the back doors.

"What's wrong?" Maggie, who'd been studying the charming brownstone buildings of Brooklyn Heights with childlike enthusiasm, pulled her eyes from the streetscape and focused on Gabriella.

"With all the craziness, I totally forgot a film crew was coming to tape Dad's acceptance speech for tonight's film industry awards. He's receiving a lifetime achievement honor for his career as a stuntman." Gabriella stared at the words on the van. "Dad, Francesco, and I were supposed to fly out to Hollywood for the ceremony, but we changed our plans after . . . well, you know. The network offered to send a film crew so Dad could accept the award remotely."

Maggie's heart hurt for Gabriella and her father. "If it's better for you, we can stay in a hotel and check back with you tomorrow."

"He's ready to meet Ina after all these years. He wouldn't be amused if I didn't take you upstairs now." Gabriella opened her car door. "We're on the top floor, but there's an elevator."

Maggie stepped into the sunshine and gazed at the brownstone, her eyes following its stately lines to the sky. Ina looked at her, probably for reassurance, and Maggie took her arm and led her into the building behind Curtis and Gabriella.

The elevator was small and slow, but Maggie was thankful for it. When the doors opened, Gabriella led them across the hall. "Welcome to our home," she said, sliding a key into a lock and turning it. She opened the door and announced, "Dad, we're here."

A film crew scurried around with stands of lights and lines of electrical cords, but Maggie was more fascinated with the room and its odd mixture of old and new. Original crown molding lined the ceiling, and hardwood floors provided a warm tone underfoot. But the open floor plan, bank of generous windows overlooking the skyline, and geometric furniture were distinctly contemporary. The fireplace mantel was polished black granite. Above it hung an exquisite poster-size photograph of a beautiful brunette woman balancing on the wing of a biplane in flight.

Maggie couldn't take her eyes off the photo and took a few paces toward it.

"My mother was beautiful, wasn't she?"

Maggie turned to see a distinguished gray-haired, bearded man resembling Sean Connery at her side. "Has anyone ever told you—"

"That I look like Sean Connery?" The man smiled with

amusement. "For decades, actually, and it brought me lots of lucrative jobs during my career."

"Oh." Maggie's cheeks burned. She held out her hand. "I'm Maggie Watson."

"Marc Valli," he said, grasping her hand as Ina walked up beside them. "And you must be my saving grace, Ina Linton."

"I don't know about that first part, but I am Ina." Ina looked straight into his eyes.

He lifted her hands to his lips and returned her stare. "I never thought I'd have the chance to thank you for saving my mother's life and mine." Tears welled in his eyes. "Thank you."

"Let's sit at the dining room table since the living room is getting wired." Gabriella walked to the sleek black table surrounded by Lucite chairs.

Marc stood until the ladies were seated, then he sat between Maggie and Ina. "Gabriella tells me you two were as responsible for finding my son's killer as the police."

"Maggie and I seem to have a knack for solving mysteries," Ina said. "I wish Alex hadn't escaped."

"Gabriella told me." Marc looked at his daughter. "The girls are in the Manhattan apartment with your mother-in-law. We've kept them out of school. Brent thought it was best for their safety."

"It was best, yes." Relief flooded Gabriella's face. "Brent is my husband. Our daughters, Lia and Bella, are twelve and fourteen years old."

Curtis's cell phone chimed, and he pulled it from his pants pocket. "I hate to cut the reunion short, but my editor wants me back in the newsroom. We need to get going so I can get these ladies to a hotel." He pushed his chair back but remained seated. "One more thing, though. Mr. Valli, Francesco was my best friend. I'd be honored if you'd allow me to finish writing your biography for him."

"I think Francesco would like that. I agree under one condition." Marc smiled, his eyes filled with emotion.

"What's that, sir?"

"You must allow the ladies to stay here tonight. Ms. Linton and I have a lot of talking to do, and we have an extra room with the girls gone." He paused. "And I want them to appear on the video with me. I wouldn't be alive to get the award if not for Ina."

"That can be arranged." Curtis broke into a grin. "As long as the ladies approve."

Maggie and Ina looked at each other, then said in unison, "We approve."

Three hours later, Maggie and Ina sat, rested and refreshed, in matching black director's chairs on either end of a white leather love seat. Marc and Gabriella sat beside each other on the love seat waiting for filming to begin. The cameraman's lights were bright and hot, but Maggie enjoyed Ina's interest in the photography equipment.

"Lighting sure has changed since I used it back in the day," Ina said, watching every move the cameraman made.

"I imagine so," Gabriella said, crossing her legs and adjusting her black beaded top.

"Suppose our friends in Somerset Harbor will see this video?" Gabriella smiled. "If they watch the awards show they will."

"We are ready to go." The director consulted his clipboard, then looked up. "Any questions?"

"We're good to go," Gabriella said.

Soon Maggie found herself in the world of lights, camera, and action. But did she really belong here? She smiled slightly, despite feeling unworthy of this recognition. *What have I done to deserve this honor?*

Marc had memorized his speech, and his words were clear and eloquent even without cue cards. After speaking for a few minutes about his life as a stuntman, he said, "It is with sincere gratitude I thank those who have made it possible for me to have the incredible career I've been blessed to experience. It has been an amazing ride, and I've enjoyed every second of it." Marc grabbed Gabriella's hand. "My daughter, Gabriella, and I are grateful for the support and respect for our family's privacy following the murder of my son, Francesco." Marc's voice broke. "But he would be proud to know his actions connected me to my past, as he spent the last year of his life attempting to do. Before I sign off, I want to introduce two very special ladies. One of them, Ina Linton, saved my life over sixty years ago. Had she not been around then, I wouldn't be here now." He squeezed Ina's hand and lifted it to his lips. "The other woman, Maggie Watson, was integral in identifying the killer of my son, award-winning journalist Francesco Valli." He reached across his daughter to Maggie, who took his hand and squeezed. "I hope you'll give them a round of applause."

By the time the director said "Cut," Maggie's eyes, like those of Ina, Marc, and Gabriella, were filled with tears. "Thank you for your kind words." Maggie blotted her eyes with a tissue from her purse. "I'm honored."

Ina hugged Gabriella and Marc. "I'm so sorry you lost Francesco, but I'm glad I had a chance to meet him and to face my past. Our past."

"Yes," Marc said. "I wish my mother had known Emil Lupei survived and that you and I would reconnect someday."

Gabriella smiled through her tears. "I think she knows."

. . . .

James and Officer Linton were the first faces Maggie saw when she exited through the security checkpoint at the Portland airport. Jaws set, eyes expectant, the men gave off an aura of tension.

"Maggie." James put his arm around her shoulder and squeezed, holding her a bit longer than usual. "Welcome home."

"I'm glad you're back, Aunt Ina," Robert said, wrapping her in a bear hug.

"Me too." Ina stepped out of the embrace and studied his face. "Okay, what gives?"

"Let's go find a quiet corner in a restaurant and talk," Robert said, looking at James.

Maggie froze. "What's going on?"

"Let me take that," James said, grabbing the handle of Maggie's rolling carry-on bag. He put his hand on Maggie's back and guided her down the corridor toward a restaurant. "It's not quite lunchtime, so maybe we'll be lucky and find a secluded table."

Queasiness rippled through Maggie. *They're both acting weird. This can't be good.*

After they'd ordered coffee and pastries Maggie was sure none of them wanted, Robert cleared his throat. "I want you to rest up today, because tomorrow I need your help."

"What do you need us to do?" Maggie's queasiness increased.

James toyed with a sugar packet. "We're going to the circus with your friends from the historical society."

"And?" Ina said in a voice laced with impatience.

Robert shifted in his seat and turned his head to scan the room. "We're hoping your presence will inspire Alex to make an appearance."

"You want us to do what?" Maggie's queasiness turned to fear.

"Are you seriously using us as bait?" Ina challenged.

"Trust me, we'll have plenty of plainclothes cops to protect you," Robert said. "We're betting Alex is hanging out at The Busy Bean disguised in a crazy getup, listening to gossip. James is going to let the word out that you two are excited to be back and use the free circus tickets donated to the historical society."

"I have a feeling she'll show up at the circus and make a move, and the police will be there when she does." James squeezed Maggie's hand. "I'd never let Robert do this if I wasn't confident he could protect you."

The conversation ceased as the waiflike waitress arrived with a tray laden with coffee cups and plates of Danish. "Enjoy your breakfast," she said, slapping the check on the table.

As if that's possible. Maggie stabbed her fork into the pastry.

Robert watched the waitress walk to another table across the dining room. "We know more about the way Alex works."

"Do tell," Ina urged.

"We found a bag full of her disguises—red, blonde, and brunette wigs, jogging gear, a man's business suit, a woman's designer suit, and assorted footwear—hidden in the spare tire well of her SUV." Robert sipped his coffee. "The car also had a few photos inside, which appear to be the ones you took in 1955, Aunt Ina. They were crumpled up in balls on the floor of the back seat."

"Alex didn't take too kindly to the photo of her grandfather assaulting Lia Cavallo," Ina said.

"I bet not," James said.

Robert cleared his throat. "And we found Francesco's laptop and Alex's cell phone with a threatening text sent to Francesco Valli minutes before he was knifed outside The Busy Bean."

The phrase *before he was knifed* echoed in Maggie's mind. "We have to do this for Francesco."

Ina nodded. "For Marc and Gabriella too. She saved us. She wanted to come back with us, but we convinced her to stay and protect her family."

Both men relaxed their shoulders. James pulled cash from his wallet and placed it on the check. "Now that that's settled, let's get out of here."

On the way to the parking garage, Maggie and Ina recounted their meeting with Emil Lupei and their reunion and video with Marc and Gabriella. After the whirlwind trip to New York, Maggie was grateful to sink into the luxurious leather back seat of James's Mercedes. She closed her eyes as Ina slipped into the seat next to her. The sounds of the men's voices in the front seat almost lulled her to sleep as James started the car and backed out of the parking space, but a nagging question urged her to open her eyes.

"I'm relieved to know who killed Francesco, and I'll be even more so once Alex is caught." Maggie tilted her head toward Ina. "But there's still one mystery I want to solve."

James groaned. "Oh no, not another one. We haven't wrapped up the murder yet."

Ina leaned toward Maggie. "Another mystery?" Her eyes sparkled. "What is it?"

"It's about you." Maggie smiled at Ina's enthusiasm. *Will she be so eager when she discovers what the mystery is?*

"Aunt Ina, you have more secrets?" Robert twisted in his seat and looked back at Ina. "What now?"

Ina shrugged. "I have no idea what she's talking about."

"Come on, Maggie." James caught her gaze in the rearview mirror. "Enlighten us."

"I've always wondered why Ina doesn't drive," Maggie said, looking at her friend. "You're one of the gutsiest, most independent women I know. Not driving doesn't seem to fit your personality."

"That's your great mystery?" Ina chuckled. "It's no big deal."

"Humor me. Please?"

"I admit I've always wondered too," Robert said.

"Oh, all right, but it's not the earth-shattering story you think it is," Ina said. "I lost interest in driving after I moved to New York City to chase my dream of becoming a professional photographer. Even back then the traffic was bad, and drivers were ill-mannered. It frustrated me."

Robert gaped at his aunt. "*That's* why you don't drive?"

"Well, yes," Ina said. "I never needed to drive when I lived in Somerset Harbor, or when I was on a college campus. By the time I moved back here from New York, walking was part of who I am. By going at my own pace, I met more people and discovered interesting places to photograph."

The car was silent for a spell. Ina pulled a face. "I told you it wasn't a big deal."

"That's not true," Robert said. "I believe Bobby and his friends would say, 'That's legit.'"

"Did you say I'm legit?" Ina held her fist up to Maggie. "That calls for a fist bump."

The two women laughed as they touched their fists together.

"Robert?" James said. "Did Maggie and Ina just do a fist bump?"

"Yeah, they sure did." Robert's laugh filled the car. "Wonders never cease."

. . . .

Maggie wasn't sure whether her fear or excitement was stronger as she stood in line inside the long red-and-white tented entrance to the Circus de Vita. Even on a day without her heightened state of awareness, the place would have incited sensory overload. Outside, an organ grinder and his monkey sidekick drew laughs from young and old alike. Inside, three crowd-control personnel dressed in gray stood on one side of the tent with their arms crossed. On the other side of the canvas passageway, a juggler inspired *oohs* and *aahs* from onlookers as he tossed five rainbow-hued clubs. The aromas of popcorn, cotton candy, animals, and women's perfume mingled in the air.

Maggie and Ina walked side by side, with Robert next to Ina and James, a newspaper tucked under his arm, beside Maggie.

"How're you doing?" Maggie linked her arm through Ina's.

"I can't get over it. The excitement and atmosphere are the

same, but everything is sleeker, bolder, and more sparkly." Ina's eyes lit up with exhilaration. "I can't believe I'm here after all these years."

Maggie surveyed the crowd. "It looks like everyone in a thirty-mile radius is here, and we haven't even made it into the big top yet. People are still streaming in."

Ina eyed the gray-clad men lined up along the side of the tent. "Lots of crowd control here. Look, there's another group behind the juggler, but their shirts say *Security*. Maybe they're undercover cops dressed as security guards."

"Maybe." Maggie panned the room. "I figured they'd use plainclothes cops in the crowd."

A few feet away, Ruth, Fran, and Liz stood shoulder to shoulder, watching the painted-face juggler toss the clubs higher and higher. Daisy was nearby talking to a young mother with a wide-eyed toddler dressed as a ballerina. Daisy broke away from mother and child when she made eye contact with Maggie and Ina.

"Isn't this fun?" Daisy threw her arms around Maggie. "I'm so glad you're back so we could all experience this together."

"We're happy to be home." Maggie yawned despite the good night's sleep she'd had while Officer Crosby kept watch outside her bedroom at Sedgwick Manor.

"I second that," Ina said. "I admit I slept better knowing Robert was right outside my bedroom door."

"I have something to show you." James unfolded the newspaper. "You two made the Portland newspaper."

Maggie looked over one of his shoulders and Ina, the other. Their faces stared back at them from the front page of the state and local section. The photo was a still shot pulled from the video filmed in Gabriella's living room. "Would you look at that," Ina said. "Makes us sound kinda important, eh?"

"Aunt Ina, you are im—"

A gasp from the crowd cut Robert off midsentence.

"Help! He hit my baby with a pin!" a woman shrieked.

Robert and James whirled toward the crowd surrounding the toddler ballerina. While the men's backs were turned, hands tugged Maggie from behind and pulled her through a small opening in the tent and outside into a small area lined with oversize vehicles.

Maggie writhed in the grasp of her captor. Wrenching her right arm free, she flailed it toward her attacker's head and knocked off the gray security uniform cap. "Let me go!" Maggie twisted in the arms of her attacker—and found herself looking into the raging eyes of Alex Lupei.

"Shut up!" Alex hissed in Maggie's ear, then threw her into the arms of a gorilla-size man in a security uniform. "Take care of her. I'll get the truck."

The large man reeked of cigarette smoke and sweat, odors that made Maggie's nose burn. She assessed her surroundings. While the entry tent had been packed with people, this spot was deserted except for the empty vehicles that blocked any potential view. *Where are the police?*

She lifted her foot and brought her heel down on the top of the henchman's shoe. When he howled, she pushed away long enough to see his face. She recognized him in an instant as Spike from the depot.

"Hold still," he growled.

Maggie stopped struggling and stared at the vehicles lined up along the fence. She caught movement between a van and a pickup truck. *Please be the police.*

"Get your filthy hands off me!" A few feet away, Ina's voice carried over the roar from inside the tent as she struggled in the grasp of another brute in a fake security uniform. He looked like the second henchman from the old depot, Mick. "Wait until my nephew gets ahold of you!"

"Ha! Your nephew is nowhere to be seen, lady." His laugh sent a shiver up Maggie's spine. "You're all alone now."

His words incensed Maggie. *How dare he talk to Ina that way!* The arms around Maggie tightened. Cigarette smoke stung her nostrils. A gun barrel was pressed against her body. Panic and anger raged through her. It had to be the police she saw among the cars. Or was it Alex?

"All alone, huh?" A smile crept across Ina's face. "I don't think so, pal."

"Freeze!" Lieutenant Yamada's voice carried across the lot as the SWAT team spilled from behind vehicles like bees swarming from a hive. "Drop your weapons and release your hostages!"

"Do it, cuz," Spike said to Mick as he thrust Maggie away from him and raised his hands in the air. "Alex will take care of everything. She always looks after family."

"Not this time," Robert said coolly, pushing a scowling, handcuffed Alex forward. Leg chains stretched between her ankles. "She's going to be tied up for a while."

Officer Crosby, standing several feet away with a stun gun held at the ready, focused her eyes on the prisoner.

"You think so?" the escape artist sneered, pulling a hand from a cuff and going for Robert's gun. With lightning speed, Crosby raised her stun gun and sent a pair of darts hurling through the air. Alex crumpled to the ground the second they hit her.

Finally, Maggie felt as though she and Ina were safe.

State police officers swarmed the area and subdued Alex's fake security team as Robert and Officer Crosby pulled Maggie and Ina out of the fray. Robert's eyes were full of emotion. "Aunt Ina, are you all right?" He bent down and hugged her. "I'm sorry I put you in such a dangerous situation."

"Oh posh." Ina stepped back and waved her hand. "This was nothing compared to Alex's knife dance around my neck. It was actually a little fun."

Robert turned to Maggie. "You were brave to act as bait. I think you're the bravest woman I know. Next to Aunt Ina, that is."

Maggie smiled despite the situation. "Now that is high praise."

Robert was called away, leaving Ina and Maggie to answer questions and be checked by paramedics. After she was given the all-clear from a medic, Maggie looked up to see James crossing the lot with a young woman in a business suit.

"Maggie, are you all right?" James hugged her tightly. He backed away and gestured toward the woman. "Maggie, Ina, this is Lorrie Sparkle, public relations manager for the circus."

"I'm glad to meet you," Lorrie said, shaking Ina's hand, then Maggie's. "Alderman Bennett told me about your history with the circus, Ms. Linton. Because of your bravery and the quick action of these officers, our matinee went on safely as scheduled. Thank you." She flashed a million-dollar smile. "This is our last day here, but if you're up to it, we'd like to give you a personal tour of the circus grounds and invite you to attend the evening show as our guests. You and all your friends, of course."

Maggie watched Ina's face register shock, but a few seconds later her eyes brightened and she smiled.

"Well, I suppose it's time to put all the fear behind me and look to the future. And I have all my friends here to experience it with me." Her eyes filled with tears. "Well, except Hattie."

Maggie put an arm around Ina's shoulders. "Let's go find our friends."

Lorrie and James led Maggie and Ina through the fence gate at the front of the circus entrance. When they entered the long tented area outside the big top, the ladies from the historical society surrounded Maggie and Ina, peppering them with questions and hugs.

"Jeez, give a girl room to breathe," Ina protested with a laugh.

As they neared the doorway into the big top, Robert tucked Ina's arm in his. "Aunt Ina, shall we finally get you to the circus?"

"Absolutely. After sixty years, the show must go on."

"You know, if you two are going to continue solving crimes," Robert said, "I'll need to talk to the chief about making you honorary police officers."

"In that case, I guess I need to think about relearning to drive," Ina said, winking at Maggie. "For right now, though, I plan to enjoy every minute of the circus tour and show."

Maggie's friends laughed and moved into the scintillating atmosphere of the Circus de Vita's big top tent.

James offered Maggie his arm.

"Don't mind if I do," she said, stifling a yawn as she slid her hand into the crook of his arm. Maggie stood still a moment as Ina entered the doorway to the tent, chattering nonstop to Robert and the ladies, white hair lifting a bit as she turned from side to side. "Look at her. She hasn't missed a beat, and here I am, yawning." Maggie's heart swelled with affection for her plucky friend.

James placed a hand over hers. "Don't be too hard on yourself. Those hardy enough to keep up with that woman are few and far between."

Maggie laughed. "Too true, Alderman Bennett."

"Shall we?" James asked.

Together, they entered the tent and let themselves be swept away by the enchantment awaiting them under the big top.